"There are lots of reasons a woman's heart races. Not all of them are good."

"Not all of them," John conceded as the music changed to a quiet sax solo. "Is it me, then? Are you afraid of this?" he asked, his thumb caressing her collarbone.

Saura's throat went dry. "I think you give yourself far too much credit, *cher.*"

"Maybe," he said. "But maybe you don't want to give me enough. Which brings me back to my question. A beautiful woman like you—" his gaze swept over her body "—why are you with a man who leaves you cold? Protection?"

The word stopped her. "What?"

"You're scared, and a rich man like him makes you feel safe."

"I'm not scared."

"Tell me something, *belle amie.*" His voice was dead quiet. "Who's going to protect you from him?"

Dear Reader,

I've always loved spring...warm breezes after months of cold, patches of green and bursts of color as trees and flowers revel in the warmth.

What better time to launch a miniseries? In MIDNIGHT SECRETS, you'll meet the Robichauds—and their childhood friends and lifelong enemies, the ties that bind and passions that burn. Along the way I'll give you a native daughter's vision of Louisiana. Katrina may have knocked us, but just like springtime, rebirth is everywhere!

Aside from my Silhouette Bombshell release, *Veiled Legacy* December 2006, it's been a while since my last Silhouette novel...and with good reason. I had a baby! It's wonderful to be telling stories again...to you, and my little girl. Would you believe she's already a storyteller herself? She lines up her dolls, sits in front of them and starts with "Once upon a time..." and always concludes with "...and they lived happily ever after!"

Sit back and let me tell you about a passionate family named Robichaud and a part of the country I adore.

Happy reading,

Jenna Mills

Jenna Mills

THE PERFECT STRANGER

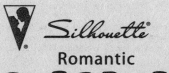

Romantic
SUSPENSE

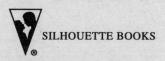

SILHOUETTE BOOKS

®

ISBN-13: 978-0-373-27531-1
ISBN-10:   0-373-27531-5

THE PERFECT STRANGER

Books by Jenna Mills

Silhouette Romantic Suspense

Smoke and Mirrors #1146
When Night Falls #1170
The Cop Next Door #1181
A Kiss in the Dark #1199
The Perfect Target #1212
Crossfire #1275
Shock Waves #1287
A Cry in the Dark #1299
*The Perfect Stranger #1461

*Midnight Secrets

JENNA MILLS

grew up in south Louisiana, amidst romantic plantation ruins, haunting swamps and timeless legends. It's not surprising, then, that she wrote her first romance at the ripe old age of six! Three years later, this librarian's daughter turned to romantic suspense with *Jacquie and the Swamp,* a harrowing tale of a young woman on the run in the swamp and the dashing hero who helps her find her way home. Since then her stories have grown in complexity, but her affinity for adventurous women and dangerous men has remained constant. She loves writing about strong characters torn between duty and desire, conscious choice and destiny.

When not writing award-winning stories brimming with deep emotion, steamy passion and page-turning suspense, Jenna spends her time with her husband, daughter, two cats, two dogs and a menagerie of plants in their Dallas, Texas home. Jenna loves to hear from her readers. She can be reached via e-mail at writejennamills@aol.com, or via snail mail at P.O. Box 768, Coppell, Texas 75019.

For my husband and my daughter,
the two brightest lights in my life.

Prologue

She watched him.

He sat alone in the far corner of the ramshackle wood structure the locals called a bar. Once, according to legend, a voodoo priestess had called the building home.

Blues music drifted across the smoky room, but the man seemed impervious to the mournful strains. An air of isolation clung to him, a palpable warning for everyone to stay away.

But Saura Robichaud kept coming back for more.

Tall and dark, he looked as though he belonged here in the backwaters of Louisiana. His grim expression indicated he did not. He looked distant, like a man who'd drawn a line between himself and the rest of the world. His hardened stare reminded her of the battered cypress trees jutting up from the swamp south of New Orleans. Sometimes she would sit and stare at the trees, wonder how much more they could endure.

She'd been watching the stranger for almost a week. Rumors swirled around him, much like the murky waters bordering the sleepy bayou town. For the most part he stayed in an old cabin on the edge of the swamp, where he sat on the porch much of the day, fishing pole in hand.

Or so rumor had it.

He didn't socialize, didn't come into town, except for a few hours each evening. More broken than dangerous, claimed the waitress who'd served his drinks—only one per night, Saura knew. He would wrap his hands around the glass and stare into the amber liquid, but she'd never seen him take a sip.

He was just passing through, the owner of the tackle shop said. The stranger who'd yet to share his name didn't want anything from anyone, save to be left alone.

For Saura, there was freedom in that knowledge, a liberation she hadn't found in a long, long time.

He didn't know who she was, didn't care about her past. She could approach him, secure in the knowledge he wasn't waiting for her to crumble. He wouldn't try to stop her, wouldn't give her a second thought when she walked away.

He looked up and caught her watching him, just as he had the past four nights. And like those other nights, her heart strummed low and hard. The moment stretched, long, thin, to the point of breaking, until he broke it, looked back down at the glass he rolled between his hands.

Saura stood. It would be easy to walk away—but she'd never been one to take the easy way out. Instead she crossed the room with a determination that had once been second nature, everything but the man in the olive T-shirt and camouflage pants fading—the sultry blues music and the pool tables, the raucous laughter. They all just slipped…away. There was only the man, and the moment. And the chance she had to take.

Last night he'd shocked her by extending a hand to her, and easing her into his arms. Against his body. They'd barely moved, had swayed to the wail of a sax. After one song she'd pulled away.

But tonight she was ready. She'd dressed in leather and brushed her hair to a sheen, dabbed expensive perfume onto her pulse points. Roses and spice. Once the bold scent had defined her. Now it seemed a garish accessory to a costume she no longer knew how to wear.

At his table she stopped, felt her heart kick hard when he glanced up. "Thought maybe I'd finally scared you off," he drawled, putting down his drink. There was a trace of Cajun to his voice. But just a trace.

Slowly, imbued with a familiarity she hadn't expected, she smiled. "It takes more than looking and dancing to run me off, *étranger.*" Stranger.

His eyes darkened. For a moment he studied her, much as a cop would scrutinize a suspect. Then he stood and reached for her wrist. His eyes remained hard, but his grip was oddly gentle. And when he spoke, his voice, low and quiet, impossibly rough, destroyed.

"How much will you give me tonight?" he asked, urging her against his body.

The scent of leather and soap and man, *of oranges,* came to her immediately, and deep inside something shifted.

"One song?" he asked. "Two?"

Somehow, she'd forgotten. Somehow she'd forgotten how solid a male body could be. How hard and warm…

The long-forgotten sensation should have made her pull back, she knew that. She should never have returned here, should never have compromised the safety of feeling nothing.

But she had to know.

One bullet.

Had it killed one, or two?

Moving against him, with him, she absorbed the feel of muscle and sinew, of strength and man. She was a tall woman, but in his arms she felt small. She had to look up to see his face, and when she did, when she saw the tarnished chain around his neck and the cleft in his chin, the urge to touch him shocked her, to lift her hand and touch. *To feel.*

Everything blurred, dimmed, once again leaving only the tall stranger with the hard eyes and gentle hands. The way he held her against his body, as if he could absorb her. As if he *needed* to absorb her. Body to body. Skin to skin. And for the first time in two years, she felt safe.

Alive.

"Keep holding me like this," she murmured against his chest, "and I might just give you three."

Chapter 1

Five weeks later

Detective John D'Ambrosia didn't do parties.

Standing near one of five bars set up throughout the elegant St. Charles Avenue mansion, he tapped his finger against the crystal tumbler, and savored the irony. For a man who religiously turned down invitations to happy hours and crawfish boils, he spent an obscene amount of time finessing invitations to parties at which he wasn't wanted.

But there was a difference. It was the man who said no. The undercover detective never overlooked an opportunity.

Surveying the room, he studied everything. The number of exits. Where each was located. If they were manned. How many security guards mingled with the guests. If they were packing.

Fifteen, he counted, including one dressed like a waiter. Others wore tuxedos, just like the other guests. Even John. The once tailored jacket hung looser than the last time he'd put it on. He'd lost weight.

He couldn't complain. His partner had lost his life.

The thought ground through him, crystallizing his attention on the elite of New Orleans. They drank and laughed and postured, while Alec lay in a crypt on the outskirts of the city. He'd been a good cop, even if in the end he'd been labeled bad. There'd been no twelve-gun salutes. No bagpipes. No convoy of police officers from parishes across southern Louisiana to pay respect.

Because dirty cops didn't get respect. They got iced.

Keeping his expression impassive, John forced his fingers to loosen their death grip on the crystal. He'd tried to do as his C.O. had instructed. Clear his head. Gain perspective. But the silence had screamed at him, and the forced vacation had given his mind too much time to wander. And the woman—

This time the crystal did shatter. Shards sliced into his palms as they fell to the parquet floor, the tonic water splashing his pants. Scowling, he closed his fingers into a fist, and felt blood.

After all this time, after all the things his hands had done, that surprised him. He would have sworn he couldn't bleed anymore.

He signaled a waiter and grabbed a wad of cocktail napkins, used them to staunch the bleeding. The woman was of no consequence. Alec was. He'd been a good man. He'd had a wife. He'd wanted kids.

Making sure his killer paid was all that mattered.

In a port city like New Orleans, black-market contraband was nothing new. But over the past six months there'd been a sharp escalation. At first mundane things, such as knockoff designer handbags and computer chips. Then a shipment of pharmaceuticals had been seized, a cancer drug that was anything but. Then came the seven dead college students with heroin in their systems, the narcotic altered somehow. Different. A hundred times more lethal.

And then there was the Russian girl found running down Tchoupitoulas. Naked. Emaciated. Beaten.

She refused to speak, not even to the soft-spoken Russian teacher from Tulane. But her eyes had flared when she'd been shown the picture of a man—the same man whose name appeared in Alec's secret files.

Now John stood in that man's home, watching him cross the extravagantly decorated den with a drink in his hand and the world at his feet. Like an actor taking the stage, the tall, deceptively elegant man moved through the adoring guests with warm smiles and polite nods. Because that's what Nathan Lambert did. Deceive, and take.

Smiling, the silver-haired man thumped a younger man on the back, kissed an older woman's hand. A younger woman put her arms around him, leaning in to kiss the sliver of his face not concealed by a wolfish Mardi Gras mask.

Nathan Lambert accepted it without missing a beat, wiped his clean-shaven cheek, then moved on.

Because that, too, was what Nathan Lambert did. Moved on. Celebrated importer by day and southern gentleman by night, the man appeared untouchable. Rumors linking him to black-market activities had circulated for years, but nothing was ever proven. Few even investigated. Especially after Lambert's only son died a hero's death in Afghanistan. In grief, he'd become as much of a martyr as his son.

John was not impressed.

With a discretion he had down to a science, he left the wadded, bloodied napkins on a serving tray and wandered to the dining room, where candles flickered from every ledge, every table. Expensive artwork hung from paneled walls, while the sound of jazz drifted in from the verandah.

The scent of roses and spice stopped him. For all of one sharp heartbeat. He turned abruptly, saw the woman. She stood on the other side of the highly-polished table, in a cluster of three other women. But removed somehow. As if she wasn't really there. A long, tight-fitting gown the color of bronze hugged her body, while Egyptian-styled feathers concealed her face.

The urge to rip off the mask moved through him with a violence that stunned.

From behind his own mask—Midnight Magic, the clerk had called it—he watched the way she dragged her finger along the rim of her wineglass, then forced himself to turn away. Her hair was auburn, not midnight. Her lips the color of blood, not that of a lover's flush. But the perfume…

Didn't matter. He couldn't spin around in circles every time he smelled the soft scent of roses and spice.

Of her.

Frowning, he plucked a stem from the tray of a passing waiter and returned to the main room, where Lambert still held court. When a woman in a red-feathered mask asked him to dance, John obliged. When another asked him to fetch a drink, he obliged that, as well. Anything to make sure he didn't stand out.

From the far side of the room, a woman came into view, and everything shifted. It was the woman from the dining room, with the mask of green, purple and black feathers, the gold sequined eye slits. This time John started toward her. Until Lambert intercepted. The older man curved a hand around her hip, shattering any possibility of this considerably younger woman being Lambert's daughter.

At least John sure as hell hoped she wasn't his daughter.

In her strappy stilettos she stood an inch or two taller than her companion. Her auburn hair was twisted behind her head to leave her shoulders bare. Actually, the dress did that. Its length sheathed her too-thin body as if someone had used a fine brush to paint the bronze over every curve—

The image slipped in before he could stop it: long, dark hair and liquid brown eyes, pale flesh and curves. It had been his hand that slid along every inch—

He crushed the memory, allowed himself only to focus on Lambert's companion. The way she smiled. The fluidity with which she moved. The way Lambert constantly kept a hand on her.

Everyone had a weakness, just as everyone had a price. And he'd bet his last dollar he'd just found Lambert's.

Now he had only to find the woman's.

The plan was so simple it almost made John laugh. Lambert had taken something from John that he could never get back.

Now, John intended to return the favor.

Everywhere she looked, she saw him. Everywhere she turned, he was there. Even when she closed her eyes—*especially* when she closed her eyes. That was when her imagination would take over, and she would find him as he'd been the last time she'd seen him, sprawled on a cot with a white sheet tangled around his hips, his olive-skinned chest and shoulders bare, his breathing rhythmic.

The urge to return to him, to slide next to him and press her body against his one more time had almost ruined everything. She'd done what she had to do. And despite the fact her plan had blown up in her face, she would not allow herself to look back. There was only forward. And Nathan.

Enjoying a moment out of the spotlight, she skimmed the rim of her wineglass along her lower lip and watched the man who could turn the future she craved into reality. He stood across the room, a tall, distinguished-looking man with thick dark hair and classic bone structure. But behind the genteel mask he showed the world, she'd caught something else in his eyes, a sadness she should have expected, but hadn't. She'd heard too many stories over the years, vicious rumors and scandalous allegations. In her mind she'd turned him into an unfeeling ogre.

But now she realized her mistake.

Nathan Lambert was a man of deep, driving passion, just like—

The thought stopped her cold. She tightened her fingers against the crystal and took a deep swallow, savored the kick of the alcohol. She refused to feel anything else, refused to let her mind drift to another man. Another night. *Another lifetime.*

It galled her that she wasn't sure which man it was who made her body burn—the man she'd loved, or the man she'd used.

Deep inside something shifted, and along with it came an awareness she'd once relied on. From behind her feathered mask she scanned the room, and saw him. The man from the dining room. He lounged just inside an arched doorway, his big body deceptively relaxed, his mask— black feathers with a red accent plume—hiding much of his face. But not the fact that he watched her. His smile was languorous as he lifted his glass toward her and held it that way—in greeting or toast or dare, she didn't know—for a long, tight moment. Then he brought the stem to his mouth and finished off his drink.

Saura felt the zing clear down to her toes.

Once she would have returned the gesture without thinking twice. Just five weeks ago she'd initiated a similar challenge. But she'd been playing by different rules then.

Now she played by Nathan's.

Or at least pretended to.

And Saura Robichaud could pretend very, very well. Especially when she wanted something. Which she did. Very, very badly.

Pretending not to notice the way the stranger still watched her, she angled her chin and looked toward the far side of the room. If Nathan still—

He was gone.

The invisible shackles that had kept her in place most of the evening vanished, and she moved quickly, working her way through the revelers, toward the hallway that ran down the center of the old house. She was a tall woman with a long stride, but the slim gown kept her steps like those of a geisha. She hurried anyway, despite the way her ankles wobbled against the obscenely high heels she'd chosen.

It had been two years since she'd worn anything other than sneakers or flip-flops.

She didn't have much time. Nathan would be back soon. He rarely left her alone for long. She had to—

"Excuse me, ma'am?"

She would have kept walking, but along with the words came the soft, cool feel of a woman's hand against her forearm. She stopped and turned, saw an older woman with a gold sequined cat-eye mask peering up at her. "I'm sorry, I was just on my way—"

"Of course you are," the woman said. "But he asked me to find you, let you know he's waiting."

Saura stiffened. "He?"

"Your date," the woman said. "He's on the patio."

The surge of excitement crystallized into something sharp and brittle. With forced politeness, she thanked the woman and made her way toward the doors thrown open to the festive patio. Music drifted in from the night, not lively and fast like the band had been playing most of the evening, but slower, more rhythmic.

The memory swept in so fast she had no time to brace herself, no time to ward off the nonexistent scent of soap and leather and man. Of sweat.

And oranges.

Then she saw him. Not Nathan. But the stranger from across the room, outside now, lounging against one of the columns supporting the verandah. As soon as she stepped outside he pushed away and started toward her.

Instinctively she turned. Nathan was waiting—

She realized her mistake too late. The older woman had not said Nathan or Mr. Lambert, as one of his guests surely would have. She'd simply said *your date.*

"Nice night," came the man's voice from behind her, and before she could lose herself in the crowd, he had a hand on her body, and she realized she had two choices: run and make a scene, or oblige him and get this over with.

Slowly, she turned, found herself looking straight into his black bow tie. "I hadn't noticed."

"That's because you're with him." His voice was low,

quiet. "You're far too beautiful to be with a man who already has one foot in the grave."

Inside everything stilled. She stared up at his cleanly shaven chin…but saw only the shadow of whiskers.

"Dance with me," he murmured, drawing her into his arms. "Let me show you what he can't."

The words were bold and arrogant, and even as she told herself to retreat, the scent of soap and leather drew her closer. Not imagined as before, but real this time. *Him.* He reached for her, slid his arms around her waist and brought her up against his tuxedo jacket, anchored her to him with a possessiveness that stunned.

"I've been watching you," he said, and the warmth of his breath feathered down her neck. Merlot, she noted as she moved woodenly against him. "All evening." Leaning back, he brought a hand to her chin, and tilted her face toward his. "You've been watching me, too."

She wanted to deny it. But couldn't. At least not to herself. "Awfully sure of yourself, aren't you—?" *Étranger.* The word jammed in her throat.

So did the sight of the cleft in his chin.

Étranger.

Denial came hot and hard and fast, but even as she grabbed at every possible reason it couldn't be true, her body sang with recognition. The familiar scent washed through her. The intimate touch. The voice. It was a little different now, more cultured than it had been in the honky-tonk, but there on its wine-tinged edges she heard the lover who'd whispered to her as he'd moved inside her, as he'd brought a hand to her face and swiped away her tears.

"Do you realize you have not smiled, not once all night?"

Her heart kicked. Denial pounded through her blood.

She had to be wrong. She'd been too careful, had targeted him with the same discipline that had once made her one of the most sought-after private investigators in New Orleans. But as she stared up at his masked face, the light of the tiki torches revealed the hard line of his jaw. The one she'd feathered her fingers against, and kissed.

The one she still touched and kissed during the long hours of the night, when he refused to stay in the shadowy cabin where she'd left him.

"And you still didn't get the hint?" she asked with the cool detachment that had always been her hallmark. "What does it take? A two-by-four to the head?"

His smile was slow, languorous. Dangerous. "Better," he drawled. "Much better."

Questions twisted through her, insane possibilities she had to consider. Maybe she'd been wrong. Maybe the man wasn't a stranger. Maybe he'd been in Bayou d'Espere for a reason. Maybe he'd been sent there. It wouldn't be the first time. People always wanted something from the Robichauds. Money. Favors. Information. Revenge.

With a cool breeze blowing against them and the sensuous jazz music weaving around them, Saura forced her body to relax, her steps to meld with his. She knew how the game was played. Once, she'd been a professional.

"But not good enough," he murmured, sliding a hand up her spine. Five weeks before, he'd unfastened her braid with an explicitness that had melted her bones, letting his fingers linger to tangle in her hair. Now he found only the bare skin at the base of her neck, and she shivered. "What are you afraid of?" he asked. "Being seen?" Slowly he extended his thumb and forefinger to circle her nape. "Being caught?"

The urge to jerk out of his arms was strong. The reality that she could not was stronger. "What makes you think I'm afraid?"

"You're in my arms, aren't you? I can feel you—see you. If you could, you would melt into the shadows." He slid his other hand lower against the curve of her back. "It's him, isn't it? Lambert. You're afraid of him."

They were just words, that was all, but with them the stranger stripped her to the bone. She was out of practice. She'd known that. But until he'd exposed her, she hadn't realized just how rusty she'd become.

"How would *you* like to see your date in another man's arms?" she asked with amazing indifference considering the twisting deep inside. Then, because he was right, she glanced toward the French doors. A dark-haired waiter stood there, but Lambert remained absent.

"Is that all you are? His date?"

Angling her chin, she shifted her attention to the man who knew things about her no other man did. For four nights she'd watched him in the honky-tonk. And for four nights he'd nursed his whiskey, not speaking to a soul. For the first two he'd not even spoken to her, not even when they'd danced in slow circles.

She wasn't sure which was more excruciating—the silence, or the third degree.

"He doesn't make you feel this, does he?" The question was low, hoarse, and for a dangerous moment she wanted to close her eyes and let go. To let the memories wash through her.

"Like how?" she asked. But as soon as she gave voice to the question, the truth seared through her. *Like more.*

His mask hid much of his eyes, but not the way they gleamed. "Like this," he said, and before she realized his intent, he lifted his hand to her chest, where her heart sang in hot, brutal recognition.

Chapter 2

Her face she could control. Her arms and her hands, her legs, her feet. She could keep her expression blank. She could keep her eyes cool. She could even keep her breathing steady. She knew how to shut things out. How to separate. How to play.

How to survive.

But beneath the skin, her ironclad control ended. Beneath the skin she'd never mastered indifference. She'd never learned to keep her blood from heating, her heart from pounding. She'd never learned to block the tingling or the wanting. The craving.

She'd never learned to stop the bleeding.

And that was where he touched her. Inside. His fingers pressed against the crushed silk of her dress, but his touch penetrated to the frenetic rhythm of her heart.

She wanted to twist out of his arms. She wanted to walk

away, walk far, as she'd done before. But running, she knew, was the best way to be chased.

And she could not let this man chase her.

Lifting her eyes, she let a slow smile curve her lips. "There are lots of reasons a woman's heart races. Not all of them are good."

"Not all of them," he conceded as the music changed to a quiet sax solo. "Is it me, then? Are you afraid of this?" he asked, letting his thumb stretch toward her collarbone.

Her throat went dry. "I'm thinking you give yourself far too much credit, *cher.*"

His thumb started to rub, softly, in a delicate rhythm her body instinctively remembered—even if his apparently did not.

She hated him for that, that he could annihilate everything inside her, while he stood there. Unmoved. Untouched.

"Maybe," he said. "But then, maybe you don't want to give me enough. Which brings me back to my question. A beautiful woman like you…" his gaze whispered over the body he'd possessed five weeks before "…why are you with a man who leaves you cold?"

The opening was too perfect not to grab.

"Maybe I'm just curious," she hedged, forcing herself to relax against him, to ignore the immediate blade of yearning. "You lured me out here. Maybe I'm just trying to find out why."

The dark flare of his eyes felt better than it should have. Body to body he stared down at her, and when she thought for sure he would have frowned, he once again smiled.

There had been no smiles the night they made love.

"You really want to know what I want?" he asked, and

the small victory she'd felt for throwing his question back into his face dissipated into a primal stillness.

It had been a long time since she'd stood on such a razor-thin line. Two men. The man from the honky-tonk, and the man who now held her. One of them wasn't real.

"How else can I decide whether to give it to you?" she asked, playing the game, even as the question twisted through her.

He slid his hand along her collarbone to her neck, where he found a few strands of hair. Auburn, not black. She knew to separate her work from her life, but when she'd dyed it before walking into Lambert's world, she'd had no idea how dangerously close the two worlds would soon brush.

"I want to know what he gives you," he said, twirling her hair around his finger. "What he does for you." Pausing, he let his eyes meet hers. "I want a chance."

He wanted more than that. The truth hovered there between them. He wanted *her,* the woman he thought was Nathan Lambert's mistress. Which meant he had no idea who she really was. *How well he already knew her.*

The realization stung. His presence in Lambert's world shattered any belief that his appearance in Bayou d'Espere had been strictly innocent. Those dark explosive hours in his cabin—

She'd thought she'd been in control. She'd thought she'd been making choices she'd never make again. All the while he, in turn, had been playing her. Using her. Nothing else made sense.

The possibilities tripped through her—he could be a reporter, looking for crumbs about the arrests that had rocked her family a few months before, the violent death of a good friend, the reappearance of a woman thought dead, the fall of someone they'd trusted. He could want to milk that, use her for an exclusive.

That was almost a comforting thought.

He could be on someone's payroll. Her family was powerful. They had enemies. He could work for someone who'd taken a hit when the Robichauds came out on top. He could have been sent to watch her family. Watch her. To gather information. To infiltrate.

He could work for Lambert.

"Excitement?" he asked, as if she'd never turned him down. Tugging her close, he spun her in a quick circle and pulled her hips to his, and dared her to lean back against his arm.

Never one to turn down a challenge, Saura met his eyes and let herself go. He held her that way, draped over his arm like silk, for a long, long moment.

Naked. It was an odd word, but exposed to him that way, with her throat and spine arched, her chest lifted, she couldn't remember the last time she'd felt more naked— not even the night in the cabin, when she had been. It had been dark then, only one candle glowing from across the room. Now an army of votives and tiki torches glimmered around them, exposing the length of her neck and the fall of her hair. Too easily he could lift a hand and—

Too easily he could see the freckles behind her ears, the ones he'd kissed and—

"That I can give you," he murmured as her heart crashed against her ribs. Abruptly he lifted her from the dip and urged her body back to his. The rush was immediate. So was the relief. And the danger.

The excitement he'd promised.

"Prestige?" There was a dark glitter to his eyes. "Not so

much. But money…money I can handle." Faces a heart-beat apart, he reached for her hand and lifted it between them, studied the diamond-crested fleur-de-lis solitaire her grandfather had given her grandmother on their fiftieth wedding anniversary. "Jewelry."

Something low and hot streamed through her. "You want to go ahead and just call me a whore?"

"Everyone has a price."

"Even you?"

He stopped moving. For a second, she would have sworn he stopped breathing. "Even me."

It was not the answer she'd expected. "Tell me then. What is it you want? Why did you trick me into coming out here?" She wanted to wrench her hand from his, but refused to give him the satisfaction. "Didn't think I'd let you touch me any other way?"

His eyes met hers. "You haven't figured that out by now?"

"If you think I'm naive enough to think this conversation has anything to do with me—"

"Protection."

The word stopped her cold. "What?"

"That's why you're with Lambert, isn't it?" He released her hand and lifted his to her face. "Because you're scared, and a rich man like him makes you feel safe."

She stilled. "I'm not scared."

"Tell me something, *belle amie.*" His voice was dead quiet. "Who's going to protect you from him?"

The question hit a nerve. "Is that what this is about?" she asked, stepping from his touch. "You want to play hero and protect the poor little damsel in distress from the big bad wolf?"

He stood very still, his eyes dark and focused one

hundred percent on her. "I know Nathan Lambert. I know what he's capable of, what he's done before."

"And yet here you are, at his party, drinking his wine." With a cutting smile, she moved in for the kill. "So tell me, just what is it you call yourself? Friend? Colleague?" She hesitated, let the sensuous strains of jazz settle between them. "Enemy?"

He didn't flinch. The breeze kept right on whispering, though, cooler than before. January rarely brought bone-chilling cold to the deep south, but it took all of Saura's willpower not to shiver.

"It's nice when relationships fit into tidy little compartments, isn't it?" he asked in that same quiet voice. "Friend or enemy." He put a hand to her neck, skimmed his fingers beneath her jawbone. "Stranger or lover."

Now she did shiver.

The change came over him so fast she almost missed it, an infinitesimal tensing of his big body, as if she'd rammed a rod into his gut. His jaw went tight and through the gold slits of his mask, she saw his eyes darken. "But it doesn't always work that way, does it?"

The question stabbed deep. The answer stabbed deeper.

"Vilify me if you want," he said, stepping away from her. "I don't want to see you get hurt. It's as simple as that."

The sense of loss surprised her. "Maybe I won't be the one who gets hurt," she shot back, ignoring the hollowness moving through her. "What would Nathan do if he knew we were having this conversation? That a friend, maybe an employee, lured me into a dance so he could warn me about him? Do you really think—"

"You won't tell him."

Keeping her gaze unaffected, she glanced toward the French doors, felt the impact clear down to her toes. Nathan stood next to the waiter with the killer cheekbones, watching them. There was a stillness to him, a readiness that jolted through like a high-octane shot. The look in his eyes—

"You sure about that?" she asked, enjoying the moment more than she should have. "Because he's standing by the doors. If you'd like to test your theory, I can—"

"Don't."

Awareness jammed in her throat. She looked up into the stranger's hard, glittering eyes, and forgot to breathe.

"No matter how much you enjoy playing, this isn't a game." Between their bodies, his hand found hers and pressed a small card into her palm. "When you need me, call."

Then he turned and disappeared among the dancing couples.

Saura glanced down and stared at the phone number on the card; tried to breathe, couldn't. Tried to think, didn't have much luck with that, either. All the pieces jangled around within her, but she couldn't make them fit.

Because of his eyes. In those final moments, she'd seen an awareness in them she'd not seen earlier—an awareness she'd not seen since he'd hovered over her in the narrow bed, and put the pad of his index finger to the moisture beneath her eyes.

He knew. Or at the very least, he suspected. Somehow, something she'd said or done had given her away.

"Dawn?"

She closed her eyes at the sound of the cultured voice, swallowed against the tightness in her throat, and pasted on a smile as she tucked the other man's business card into her purse. Then she turned. "Nathan."

He took her hand and drew her wrist to his mouth for a soft kiss. "Miss me?"

"Of course," she said with the demureness countless etiquette coaches had drilled into her.

His eyes warmed briefly, before darting toward the side of the verandah. "Who was that man?"

The question gave her one of the answers she'd been seeking. Whoever he was, Nathan did not know him. Unless that, too, was part of the act. "I'm not sure." She snagged a bacon-wrapped shrimp from a passing waiter and popped it into her mouth. "We didn't get to names."

Nathan took her free hand and frowned. "You okay? You look a little pale."

She didn't hesitate. She'd missed her opportunity earlier, when Nathan had vanished from the party. "Just a headache," she said, and for effect lifted a hand to her temple. "I shouldn't have had the red wine—"

He reached for her elbow. "Let me get you some aspirin."

"Thank you." She let her eyes warm with gratitude. "But I've got some in my purse. What I could really use is a quiet room…"

From behind a boxwood hedge at the far side of the verandah, John watched her. He held his cell phone toward the makeshift dance floor, moving it slightly to keep her in his screen. She laughed. She smiled. She let Lambert touch her.

Much as she'd let John touch her five weeks before.

His blood boiled. Deception stung. Both reactions surprised.

From the moment he'd walked into Lambert's Garden District mansion, he'd sensed her. Because of the perfume, he'd told himself. Because of the scent of roses and spice that had assaulted him as he'd moved through the old house.

But now he knew. His imagination wasn't playing tricks on him. He wasn't getting soft. The woman was real, and she was here, and she was involved with Lambert clear up to her pretty lying eyes. In the small bayou town, those same brown eyes had slayed him. She'd looked at him from across the shadowy honky-tonk, and damn near eviscerated him. A stranger.

The reaction had almost sent him for the door. Instead, he'd watched her walk toward him, watched her reach out a hand. And like a fool, he'd stood and taken her into his arms. For three nights. Then he'd taken her into his bed.

All because of those aching, damaged eyes. They'd spoken to him of a pain he wanted to forget, a pain he should have left alone.

Pushing the small button, he captured her image. Again, and again, and again. It's what he should have done all along. Take her picture, check her out. Find out why she'd been in Bayou d'Espere. If he'd been her target all along, sloppy seconds—or some other means to an end.

"I've got something for you," he said, when Gabe Fontenot's voice slurred through the crackle of the cell phone. Drinking, John figured, and felt the quick whip of guilt. He'd been so obsessed with his own crusade, he hadn't called Gabe in weeks.

Of course, Gabe didn't answer the phone much these days, either.

"I need you to check something," he added.

"If I can," his friend said. "But you know I'm not back at the courthouse yet."

John frowned. Two months had passed since the celebrated assistant district attorney had torn through the woods south of town, only to find a gun pointed at his heart.

When the smoke cleared, the assailant was not the only one whose life had been blown to bits.

"Nothing official," John explained. Gabe was a Robichaud by birth. He had the connections to ask around, see if anyone recognized the woman. Who else she might have targeted. What information she might have seduced her way into. "Her hair is auburn in the picture, but I've seen it black." Like midnight rain.

"I'll see what I can do," Gabe said as John stabbed at the buttons to upload the images.

"Let me know," he said, then disconnected the call. Flipping his phone shut, he watched Lambert put a hand to his lover's back, then lead her through a trail of tiki torches toward the house.

Questions twisted with frustration. And suspicion. The woman had given no indication that she recognized him, but he found that hard to believe. His mask didn't hide his features anywhere near as well as her hair color and makeup disguised hers. If anyone should have been in the dark, it was him.

Which meant she was playing him. Hoping he didn't recognize her. Scrambling to preserve her game.

Slipping the phone into an inside pocket, John rounded the verandah and took the steps, strode toward the house. Along the way he plucked another glass of wine.

If the lady wanted to play, he could play.

A Louis XV king-size bed dominated the masculine room. With an intricate crest carved into the curved head and footboards, the bed was what Saura would consider a statement piece. An antique, she figured. Made of walnut. Definitely plantation vintage.

She would expect nothing less of Nathan Lambert.

Closing the door, she leaned back and enjoyed a moment of satisfaction. Men could be so gullible. They saw what they wanted to see. Believed what they chose to believe. As a little girl that fact had broken her heart. As a woman, the reality of it had become her saving grace.

She no more had a headache than she had auburn hair.

Four weeks had passed since she'd rented a row house on the outskirts of the Quarter, and gone after Nathan. At the first party, a fund-raiser for Hurricane Katrina reconstruction sponsored by the historical society, she'd positioned herself so he would bump into her, spill her drink on them both. It had been quite an introduction.

A week later, celebrating New Year's at Preservation Hall, she'd coyly looked away whenever he caught her watching.

At the third party, days later to kick off Mardi Gras season, he'd asked her to dance. The man she'd hired as her date had done an admirable job of appearing jealous, but in the end, he'd let her go, and contact was made.

There'd been seven dates since then. Nathan had taken her to lunch three times. They always had a private table. Once, he'd treated her to a private dining room. There were always flowers. And a tenderness that had surprised her.

If she'd not known him for the murdering bastard he was, she might have fallen under his spell. As it was, she'd enjoyed herself enormously—at least she had when she'd not been thinking about another man who'd shown her unexpected tenderness.

Saura pushed the unwanted thought aside and got to work, went first for the bed. From her purse she retrieved surgeon's gloves and snapped them onto her hands. Then she went for the mattresses. It was a rudimentary spot, but it never ceased to amaze her how many smart, resourceful people did dumb things like keep bearer bonds under their pillows or blackmail photographs in a cookie jar.

That all seemed like another lifetime now. She'd been younger then. Naive. She'd not known what it was to love, or to lose. She'd not known what it was to look at the world and see only glaring shades of white. To walk in the sunshine and feel only the cold. To eat chocolate and taste nothing. To spray on so much perfume others gagged, while she smelled nothing.

Nathan's room smelled of tobacco. Not cigarettes, but sweeter, like that from the pipe on the walnut nightstand, next to a dense hardback about famous generals of the Civil War. Out of habit she flipped through the pages, made sure no secret compartments lurked inside. Once, she'd found a small red address book hidden in such a way, and with its contents, she'd made her client very, very happy.

Femme de la Nuit, she'd been called then. Lady of the Night. And she'd been the best. Socialite by day, private eye by night, no one ever made the connection, not even her police detective brother.

Now most people thought she was dead.

Enjoying the once familiar rush, Saura finished off the bed and checked out the nightstands. After slipping a few small discs in inconspicuous places, she looked toward the armoire across the room. Just beyond stood a dressing chair and the door to the white bathroom. On the marble counter inside, she saw a folder.

Wasting no time, she hurried in and started to photograph, froze when the sound of a door opening broke the silence.

Slowly, she stepped back from the mirrored vanity and slipped the small camera into her handbag. Nathan expected her to be in bed, but she could come up with any number of reasons to be in the bathroom. She could even position herself on the floor and blame the migraine.

It had worked before.

The door opened with a slight creak, but Nathan's Bruno Maglis did not sound on the wood floor. Not even softly. And as she stood shielded by the bathroom door, she muttered a silent thanks for the genius of his decor. Typically one would think wood flooring too austere for a bedroom. But the long planks boasted an advantage carpet did not. It would not absorb footsteps. Unless someone was very, very careful.

There was no reason for Nathan to be careful in his own bedroom. Unless, of course, he sought to take Saura by surprise.

Several seconds of punishing silence passed before she heard the door close. But she did not move, did not for one second think she was alone.

"I know you're in here," he said, and her heart almost stopped. "Your perfume gives you away."

Chapter 3

The voice whispered through her on a violent caress. She stood so acutely still, not trusting herself to move, to so much as breathe. He could be anywhere. Just inside the door. At the bed. Nearing the bathroom. And if he found her—

Her hand closed into a tight fist. She practiced yoga four times a week and had stayed current with tae kwon do, but it had been two years since she'd had a sparring partner. It would only take one lightning move for him to remove her mask—and expose her lies.

Her perfume. The mistake burned. She'd colored her hair and changed her makeup, but she'd overlooked selecting a new perfume. She was rustier than she realized. Scent, after all, was the sense most strongly correlated with memory.

"You don't need to hide from me," he said in a dangerously quiet voice that made her blood sing. "I'm not here to hurt you."

She stiffened. Curiosity tempted. Very slowly, she shifted so that she could see through the crack between the door and the wall, and saw him. The big bed should have made him look smaller. It didn't. Standing to the left of it, with his bow tie unfastened and hanging against the stark white of his shirt, the top several buttons unfastened to reveal his throat and a hint of the dark hair covering his chest, he looked very much like a man about to strip down and climb into bed.

In one hand he held a crystal goblet with burgundy liquid. In the other hand—a plume of black and red feathers.

Shock seared her throat. He stood there completely exposed, as if he had absolutely nothing to hide from her.

"I understand why you don't trust me," he said. "After the way I came on to you." He lifted the glass to his mouth and threw back the rest of his drink. "That's why I'm here. To apologize."

Her mind raced. He sounded sincere. He sounded remorseful. But she also knew the cat usually did, right before he pounced.

"I came on too strong," he said. "I know you're with Nathan."

The sight of him lingering by the big bed threw her back to another night, another bed. When only a candle had lit the room. But she'd seen him anyway, every inch of him as she'd tugged at his clothes. Almost feverishly she'd run her hands along his body, driven by the warmth of his flesh. For so long there'd been only cold…

He'd been hot tonight, too. When they'd danced. When she'd forced her arms to curve around his body, to endure the feel of him, the strength and the memory.

Swallowing hard, she ignored the sight of his hand lingering against the sheets, and toyed on the pieces. Two years before, her brother's life had been blown to bits. He'd been hunted and persecuted, condemned and outcast. At the time, she'd been unable to help him. Then, two months ago, he'd been vindicated. But in the process her dear friend Alec had been killed, and Nathan Lambert had vowed he'd not yet played his last card.

Only a few days later the stranger arrived in the out-of-the-way bayou town, his clothes as battered as his eyes. Now here he was, at Nathan Lambert's party. In his bedroom. Apologizing to *her.*

"It's because of your perfume." With the quiet words he turned toward the bathroom, and her heart slammed hard.

She'd forgotten. In the five weeks since she'd run her fingers along his face, she'd forced herself to forget how brutally handsome he was, how a man could look so untouchable and lost at the same time. But now she saw, and now she remembered.

And damn him, now she wanted.

She wanted to go to him, touch him again, pretend they were two different people, in one very different situation, to skim her finger along his cheekbone to his mouth, along his lower lip—

"It sounds crazy, but for a minute there I thought you were someone else. There was a woman," he said, and her throat went dry. "We were only together once, but I can't get her out of my mind. I made her cry."

Saura stiffened. Logic, she told herself. Indifference. No matter what the stranger said, the truth could not be changed. He was here. In Nathan's world. And even though Nathan denied knowing him, she knew better than to accept everything she was told, everything she saw, at face value.

Only a stupid man publicly shared drinks with informants and assassins.

People lied, but facts did not. The man had been in Bayou d'Espere, and now he was here. Which meant he was involved. It wouldn't be the first time someone infiltrated her family. People she loved had been hurt. One was still missing after over a decade. Another lay dead.

All of them she intended to avenge. Because no matter who this man really was, who he worked for, he'd made one critical mistake.

Saura Robichaud was no one's weakness.

"She left me," he was saying. "Without saying goodbye."

Saura closed her eyes.

"She thought I was asleep, but I wasn't." With the words, he turned toward the bathroom. "I felt her get out of bed, watched her put on her clothes and run for the door."

Saura bit down hard—she had not *run* for the door. She'd walked. Very slowly. Very deliberately.

"She was scared. I could tell something was wrong. That's why I didn't go after her. She wanted away from me."

The memory scraped clear down to the bone. She hadn't been afraid. She'd been stunned.

"I tried to let her go," he said, and like a predator, began to move. With silence. With stealth. "I told myself it was what she wanted. What she deserved. But I couldn't do it. I couldn't just lie there and let her walk away, not after the way she'd touched me."

The walls of the glowing white bathroom closed in on her. Questions wove through her like a razor-fine needle. Shifting slightly, she pulled herself deeper behind the open door. With a few more steps, he would be inside.

"I went after her," he said. "Tried to find her."

A game, she reminded herself. Just a game. And while she loved playing, she never allowed herself to be the mouse. The man didn't mean a word of what he was saying. He was only trying to lull her into a false sense of security.

"But I never found her," he said, stepping onto the white marble title. "Until tonight."

She sucked in a sharp, silent breath.

"I walked into Nathan's house, and despite the candles and cloud of expensive perfume, I smelled roses. And spice. And I knew she was here."

Saura gritted her teeth. Next time she would choose something softer. Like powder and vanilla.

"Then I saw you."

Holding herself viciously still, she watched him move deeper into the spacious bathroom, glancing at the glass-block shower, then doing a sweep of the toilet room and linen closet.

"And touched you," he went on, edging toward the open closet at the back of the bathroom. "But in my mind it wasn't you. It was her. The woman I've been looking for." He put a hand to the knob, and pushed. "Because of your perfume."

Once she might have believed him. Even now, part of her wanted to. So badly. To know his words were from the man, for the woman. Not part of the game.

But that was a mistake she could not make. She'd picked him for a reason, she reminded himself. Because he was a stranger. Someone who could not touch her. Could not hurt her.

His words, his lies, did not matter.

Holding her breath, she watched him step into the darkness

of Nathan's closet. Only then did she move. Carefully, she stepped from behind the door and slipped into the bedroom. Lifting the dressing chair, she carried it to the bathroom.

And pulled the door shut.

In total, no more than six seconds passed.

She knew the second the stranger realized her intent. She heard him swear creatively, heard the sound of his expensive dress shoes come down against the marble. But by then she'd wedged the chair under the doorknob.

"Don't do this!" he roared, jerking at the door.

But Saura only smiled. All that discipline. All that smooth talking and those buttered rum words. Empty. Lies. All of them.

"Maybe this time you'll get the hint," she whispered, then turned and for the second time, walked away.

John didn't do smiles any more than he did parties. But standing there in the obscenely white, mausoleum-like bathroom, he felt his mouth curve.

Some things were just too easy.

Mission accomplished, he strolled toward the window and eased it open, climbed over the ledge and into the night.

His foray into Nathan Lambert's world had just gotten a hell of a lot more interesting.

I couldn't just lie there and let her walk away, not after the way she touched me.

The words stayed with Saura long after she made her excuses to Nathan and drove away from his St. Charles Avenue mansion. Far too restless to crawl into bed, she swung by the new little house that didn't yet feel like a home, shrugged out of her dress and heels and into jeans, an old flannel shirt and sneakers, then locked up and slipped into the night.

She'd always loved New Orleans, had started sneaking up to the Quarter when she was only fourteen. Maybe if her parents had been alive, someone would have noticed. But her uncles had been busy men, without a single clue how to handle a teenage girl. Hormones, makeup, drama, broken hearts and designer jeans had been as foreign to them as complacency was to her.

By the time she was fifteen, she'd become as familiar with the streets of the *Vieux Carre* as her brother was with the swamps surrounding their home. She'd learned where to go and where not to go, whom to trust and whom to avoid. How to slip by unnoticed. And just how valuable invisibility could be.

Now she walked those same streets, a stranger in a once-familiar world. To the untrained eye, much looked the same. The fabulous old buildings with their balconies and ironwork, the bushy hanging baskets of ferns and petunias even in the dead of winter. A few hours before the balconies had been crammed with Mardi Gras revelers. Now, with the hour pushing close to 3:00 a.m., there was only a wistful stillness and the smell of stale beer.

The names of several bars were new. Old man Pitre had passed away, and his heirs had sold The Easy Note to investors from New England. They hadn't changed a thing physically, but the second she'd walked inside, she'd felt the difference. Around the corner Madam Picou's bakery still served beignets every morning, but the woman who'd once greeted Saura with big-bosomed hugs now stared blankly at her. Alzheimer's, a clerk explained. The lovely old Creole woman didn't know her own daughter from a random tourist, but she still insisted on coming to work every day.

Passing the bakery, Saura lifted a hand to the darkened window and smiled against the tightening in her throat. Life moved on. People came and went. Memories were the only thing that remained the same. Or so she'd once believed.

Now, even memories played tricks and games.

Every night since her return, she'd walked these streets, as if in doing so she could somehow go back. Fit in again. Erase all that had happened and find a way to move forward.

But there was no erasing. The only way to get what she wanted was one methodical step at a time. Starting with Nathan Lambert.

And the stranger.

His presence in Nathan Lambert's world changed everything. She could not move as freely as she'd been doing for the past several weeks. She'd have to be more careful. Rely more on private time with Nathan than that in the company of others.

In all likelihood, the man who'd tracked her into Nathan's bedroom was, in some way, affiliated with him. He'd arrived in Bayou d'Espere for a reason—a reason he may have thought he'd accomplished by taking Saura to bed.

A reason she'd thwarted by walking away.

Two years had passed since she'd worked to connect dots, but her instincts remained sharp. And they screamed that while she and the stranger had held each other on the dance floor, he'd recognized her—*it's because of your perfume*—but didn't want her to know.

It was that thought which nagged at her as she took the three steps to her porch and slid the key into the door. She stepped inside and flipped on the light, saw the woman sprawled beneath the gold afghan on her sofa. Once, the sight would not have surprised her. She and her brother's fiancée had shared everything.

But the woman sliding tangled blond hair behind her ears and squinting up at Saura had been called Savannah then. And her brother Adrian had been alive.

Now she was called Renee, and Adrian was dead.

"What time is it?" Renee asked in a raspy voice Saura hadn't gotten used to yet.

She closed the door and turned the lock, ignored the way her throat tightened. When she looked at Renee she still saw the face of a stranger, but her heart recognized the friend who'd survived a brutal attack and made her way back to those who loved her.

"It's late," she said, tossing her purse and keys into a chair. Because the words came out harsher than she'd intended, she softened them with a smile. "I'm thirsty," she said, walking to the kitchen. "Want anything?"

"No, I'm fine."

Saura grabbed a bottle of water from the fridge and un-screwed the cap, took several sips as she returned to the front room. "Where's Cain?"

Renee rolled her eyes. "The official story or the truth?"

Saura glanced at a clock tucked beside a potted ivy on a shelf near the window. Her brother had been off the force for two years, but that didn't mean he stood on the side-lines. "It's a little late for poker or pool," she commented.

Which meant he was playing another game.

"Bingo," Renee said. Her skillfully reconstructed face was different, but the exasperation in those catlike eyes was the same. "He dropped me off a little while ago, said he'd rather me crash here than alone in a hotel."

"Don't you mean babysit?" Saura wanted to feel anger over that. But couldn't.

Renee's smile tightened. "He worries about you. We all do."

Saura shrugged that off. "How long have you been here?" It had been a little before midnight when Saura had stopped by to change clothes. "Isn't it a little late for surprise visits?"

Renee had the grace to flush.

"I know, that's what I told him. We were at Beauregard's and he got a call, said he needed to go. I'm betting it was Gabe. He's been worried about him."

Frowning, Saura looked from Renee to the old rosewood secretary she'd picked up for a song at a local antique shop. But she did not allow herself to look through the glass doors, did not allow herself to see a thirteen-year-old Gabe grinning back at her through the shadows of time. But she saw anyway, just as she always did. Dressed in swim trunks, her lanky cousin had one hand outstretched in the peace sign, his other draped around his little sister. Cain clowned around in the background. Laughing, Saura had taken the shot.

Only a few days later all that carefree innocence had been shattered by one well-placed bullet.

"I stopped by his house this morning." King cake in hand, she'd hoped to get him to open up to her, answer a few questions. "But he didn't answer the door."

"Was he home?"

"Not sure. His car was there, but the house was dark."

Renee let out a deep breath. "He breaks my heart."

Saura's, too. She took another sip of water and sat on the edge of an old floral wing chair, toed off her sneakers.

"I—" She glanced at the picture, decided against saying anything prematurely. "I might know a way to help him." If only Saura could find the one person who could make a difference to Gabe—if only she was alive.

"But you're not going to tell me."

"Not yet."

Renee drew her knees up against her chest and studied Saura, as if trying to decide how hard to push. An investigative reporter by training, her friend was not one to take no for an answer—unless she wanted something in return. "You okay?" This time her voice was softer. "You seem…distracted."

"Just tired," Saura started to deflect, but something stopped her. For almost two years there'd been no one. Savannah had been gone, Adrian dead, Cain in his own private hell. In the space of only a few months she'd lost them all. And during that time, she'd forgotten. She'd forgotten what it was to share. To give and to take. To sit up late at night, with hot chocolate and bottles of toenail polish, trading gossip and making plans.

But now—the realization of just how badly she wanted it all back closed like a fist around her throat.

"There was this man." Just saying the words felt odd, like taking off a pair of dark sunglasses and bracing for the harsh light of the sun. "A few weeks ago. At Lucky's."

Renee leaned forward. "A man?"

Saura was a thirty-two-year-old woman. She was single. She'd never shied away from risk—or opportunity. The fact there'd been a man should not have made an odd light glimmer in her friend's eyes. "A stranger," she clarified. "He pretty much kept to himself." Except for close to three explicit hours. Then he'd done anything but keep to himself. "Do you remember hearing anything? Maybe Cain said something?"

"Unless he works for Lambert, I'm afraid I'm drawing a blank."

Saura stiffened. "Lambert?"

"Cain thinks he had something to do with Alec's death."

The low buzz started within her. Saura knew what her brother and her uncle thought—she'd overheard them several times. She'd seen their file. That was a big part of why she'd come to New Orleans.

Alec Prejean had been her friend. He'd also been her brother's partner before Cain had been forced to leave the NOPD. In the months before Alec's death, his life had spun out of control in ways Saura would never forgive herself for not noticing. She owed it to him to find out what had gone wrong, and who'd lured him to his death.

"Do they have any evidence? Anything to go on?"

"Nothing concrete. Lambert threatened Edouard after I came back to town, vowed he wouldn't go down without a fight. Edouard's been edgy ever since."

That wasn't the only reason her uncle had been edgy. Saura still couldn't believe he'd let the only woman he'd ever loved pack up and move away. But he had. Said it was for the best.

"…ask Cain," Renee was saying. "See if he's heard anything about a stranger poking around."

"Don't worry about it," Saura said, standing. She had enough to go on. In only a few weeks she'd established an in with Lambert, and now, thanks to the file on his bathroom counter, she had an address. She needed only the sunrise to see what else she could find. Alerting her brother to the fact she'd noticed the stranger would get her nowhere. She was a skilled investigator. She neither needed nor wanted her hand held.

Or kissed.

The thought jarred her. "Chances are he was just passing through," she said, finding a yawn and stretching. "We can talk more in the morning. It's late and I'm exhausted. We should—"

"Saura?" Dead serious, Renee stood and crossed the room, stooped and picked something up from beside Saura's chair. "Care to tell me about these?"

Saura stared at the strappy stilettos, not that different from shoes she'd once owned, but light years beyond the sneakers and flip-flops she'd worn for the past two years. And Renee knew it. "A girl's entitled—"

"And your hair?" Renee reached out to twirl an auburn strand around her finger. "You didn't really think I wouldn't notice, did you?"

The slow, silly smile surprised her. So did the urge to pull the woman who'd once been her best friend into a hug. It's what she would have done before. Tease Renee, parcel out just enough information to make her crazed with curiosity, then laugh and give her an air kiss, flounce away.

Now Saura felt her face go tight, something jagged lodge in her throat.

Renee dangled the stilettos. "Two plus two are adding to one very interesting—"

Saura snatched the shoes. "Two and two add to four," she said with an abruptness that surprised her. But she couldn't stop it. "Not everyone can go back," she whispered as Renee's eyes went dark, and this time her voice broke. "For some of us, there's only forward."

Renee's hand fell away from her hair. "Saury, I'm sorry—I didn't mean, it's just sometimes I forget—"

"Well, I don't." Saura refused to let her voice break again. Refused to let herself break. "I *can't.*" With that she turned and headed down the hall, left Renee standing there.

Only after she closed the bedroom door did she allow herself to pull the blanket from her bed and wrap it around herself as she fired up her laptop.

But she didn't stop shaking.

He came to her in her dreams, just as he had every night since they'd made love. But this time she saw the hard glitter in his eyes. She felt the possessiveness in his touch. And this time, she pulled away.

Ignoring the tightness in her chest, Saura passed an old five-and-dime on Canal Street. A cool breeze blew off the river, but hunched down in a bulky New Orleans Saints jacket, she did not feel the bite—and she no longer shook.

I tried to let her go…

Before in her dreams, he'd said nothing. Only watched her. And reached for her. Touched her. And loved her with a raw intensity that left her damp and tangled in her sheets. But this time, in those brittle predawn moments before she'd pulled herself awake, there'd been words.

…but I couldn't do it…

Pulling the baseball cap lower, Saura waited with a group of tourists and locals for the light to turn green. New Orleans was a city that stayed up late and woke up early, vibrating with too much life and vitality to stay still for long. Not even Katrina had changed that.

…couldn't just lie there and let her walk away…

The words followed her across the street, much as they'd

whispered around her in the shower. But now she ignored them and lifted a cardboard-wrapped paper cup of *café au lait* to her mouth, savored the rush of warmth down her throat.

By the time she reached the abandoned five-story building on Prytania, the man was barely more than a hazy memory. There was only the burn of excitement, the surety that somewhere within the red brick walls, she would find what she needed to make sure Alec Prejean had not died in vain.

Only a few blocks from the elegance and charm of St. Charles Avenue, the old hotel looked lost. Abandoned. Like an old woman in a faded dress. You had only to look in her eyes to see the echoes of her youth, and know that once she'd been beautiful.

But now darkness bled from her windows, and boards barred the once-grand entrance. Broken bottles and empty fast-food wrappers littered the crumbling mortar at her foundation. Even the wrought iron shutters and columns were chipped and peeling. *Le Vieux Maison,* she'd been called during her last incarnation. The Old House. Once, the name had charmed. Now, with the hotel abandoned for nearly ten years, the name seemed sadly appropriate.

Easing along the side, Saura made her way to the back and found the door barred shut. But the windows were another story. She put a gloved hand to one with two broken panes, and lifted.

Mold and dust and bourbon hung like a rancid perfume in the stale air, and as Saura made her way through what had once been a kitchen, she would have sworn she smelled coffee and roses.

But that was impossible.

The shadows pulled her deeper into the cool stillness. The furniture had all been removed, the only remaining artwork was the graffiti scrawled over faded murals and peeling plaster. Near the main staircase, against a curved banister with broken spindles, someone had airbrushed a Spanish-moss infested live oak.

Saura swallowed hard, told herself she did not hear music. Could not hear music. That was only her imagination. As was the lingering scent of soap and leather.

Abandoned buildings had a feel to them, she knew. Old warehouses and factories, hospitals, plantations, even something as benign as a gas station or fishing shack, they all shared the same heavy silence. Long after the last occupant walked out the door, the buildings remained. Waiting. Day after day. Month after month. Year after year. Fading in the sun.

Tracing her hand along the tree, she kept close to the wall as she edged toward a door at the end of the narrow hall.

He wasn't alone.

John slipped back into the stairwell and eased the door shut, held himself motionless as he listened. Footsteps coming down the warped wood planks of the fourth-floor hallway. Soft. Light. Cautious.

The stillness bled through him, the way it always did in those raw moments when just one wrong breath could be his last. Slowly, he reached for his Glock, curved his finger around the trigger, and waited.

From the moment he'd stepped inside the old hotel, he'd known he wasn't alone. But then, he hadn't expected to be. That was why he was here. Because of the address he'd seen jotted on a piece of paper in Lambert's folder.

From outside, the squeal of tires broke the silence. As brakes screeched, John reached for his walkie-talkie, but before he could contact his friend standing lookout, glass shattered somewhere nearby.

And the footsteps stopped.

"Sweet Christ," came the scratchy voice through his headset. "Pull back, pull back!"

"What the hell?" John roared, but already he smelled smoke. And the footsteps turned into a hard, dead run.

On blind instinct he threw open the stairwell door and lunged into the hallway. Smoke engulfed him, as greedy red flames licked at the rotting woodwork.

John barely recognized the snarl that ripped from his throat. He was close, damn it. So close to finding—something…something Lambert would rather destroy than risk falling into the wrong hands.

"Get out of there, man!" But John didn't move. Couldn't move. "The place is a freaking tinderbox!"

Through the smoke he saw her. Running toward him. Coughing. Stumbling.

Falling.

"No!" he roared, lunging, but then the voice of reason shouted in his ear.

"Pull back! Not much more time!"

She wasn't there. He knew that. She'd never been there, not in the smoke, not in the shadows of his imagination.

Throat burning, he squinted through the growing darkness—and saw nothing. Heat blasted him. Somewhere nearby a wood beam crashed. And another. A wall collapsed, and flames licked into the hall.

Coughing, he spun and pulled open the stairwell door, lunged into the darkness and down the steps, fought to breathe.

This time, she wasn't getting him killed.

Chapter 4

The smoke punished. Thick gray clouds swirled through the fourth-floor hall, stinging Saura's eyes and her throat. She squinted and tried to see, to breathe. Couldn't. The fire consumed the oxygen at an alarming rate, leaving only toxins to singe her throat. Coughing, she dropped to her hands and knees and crawled, knew smoke killed more people than fire.

And she would not be one of them.

Eyes stinging, she reached for the doorknob and found it warm, not hot, knew it was safe to go in. If the fire burned inside, the glass would have blistered her hand. With a quick shove she gained access and slammed the door behind her, tried to gain her bearings through the dense smoke. Crawling for the window, she stripped off her jacket and grabbed at her T-shirt, pulled it over her head and wadded it into a ball. Just as quickly she slipped the jacket back on and reached for her backpack, pulled out a bottle of water and poured it onto the fabric. Then she brought it to her mouth and breathed.

Five minutes. Maybe seven. That's how long she had before the room went up in flames.

Nostrils burning, she used her hands to guide her, felt the large crate. And another. And another. Four of them before she reached the window. With the door closed it was safe to pull it open, let oxygen flow inside.

But the wooden ledge would not budge.

Gasping, she lifted a leg and kicked out a pane. "Help!" she shouted against the roar of the fire. "Help!"

But there was no one to hear.

In the distance, sirens sounded above the hissing, but the realist in her knew help would never arrive in time. The smoke thickened with each second. She fought it, kept her face to the window, but her vision blurred, and the fuzziness pushed closer.

She heard the groan too late. Twisting, she lifted her arms to shield her as the beam crashed inches from her legs. Heat poured in on the boiling air, bringing with it the outer bands of the fire. She scrambled backward, said a prayer. "No!"

There would be no rescues, she realized in some hazy corner of her mind. No firefighters storming through the door. No net to catch her when she jumped.

No strangers with hard eyes and gentle hands.

In her mind she could see him, much as she'd imagined him minutes before, lunging for her. Running. Shouting…

Blinking at the illusion, she knew it was starting. Her mind, starved for oxygen, was beginning to play tricks. Her body, slowly shutting down. Refusing to let go, she realized she no longer had a choice. She had to jump.

But the fire had other ideas. On a greedy rush, it raced toward the supply of oxygen and licked out the window, blocking her escape. Blindly, she spun for the door, saw only smoke as the flames drove her to her knees. She crawled until she found the door, reached for the knob. She would not give up. She could not—

Smoke awaited her. It licked and curled and consumed—

But then he was there, emerging through the gray and shouting. Coughing. Swearing.

She could make out no detail, only that he reached for her, pulled her into his arms and over his shoulder, held her tight as he spun and started to run.

He didn't care who she was. Didn't care what she was doing there. Who she worked for. He only knew that she was real, and she'd been trapped in the building.

He'd tried to tell himself he was only imagining things. He'd gotten as far as the second floor before he'd bolted back up the stairs. If there was even a razor-thin chance anyone was trapped, he could not leave them to die.

And then he'd opened the door and run through the haze, saw her.

Now he coughed against the thick smoke and took the stairs two at a time. The heat pushed down on him. The lack of oxygen made him dizzy. Battling it, he shifted her in his arms, shifted her out of the firefighter's hold so that he cradled her, could use his body to shield her if anything fell.

"John! Where the hell are you?"

No time to answer. He pulled her closer and kept running. She was light in his arms, clinging to him with an intensity that surprised him. After the way she'd fought to survive, he would have expected her to collapse. To go limp and pass out. But she did none of that. She held on like a lover in the heat of passion and buried her face against his throat.

"Hang on!" Rounding the last corner, he ran down the steps and kicked open the door.

The smoke was less intense down here, the temperature at least thirty degrees cooler. He could see again, and he could almost breathe. But still he ran, even as he heard the fire engines. They would arrive any minute. With them, the police.

He could not let them find him—or her. Neither of them belonged there.

Against him she coughed, forcing him to realize how tightly he held her face to his jacket. He carried her through the kitchen and pushed open the rear door, staggered into the chill of early morning.

"Breathe!" he told her, but barely recognized the rough edge to his own voice. *"Breathe."*

"Look! Someone's coming out!" he heard a man shout, but he kept running against the burn of his throat and his eyes, his muscles. She shifted again, dislodging the baseball cap pulled low over her head.

And a long, dark braid tumbled against his arm.

He felt himself stagger, felt himself recover as he rounded another corner and darted into a quiet side street. All the while the braid swayed against the leather of his jacket, and burned clear down to the bone.

Possibilities pushed in from all directions. She'd set him up. She'd left the calendar on Lambert's counter on purpose. She'd lured him to the old hotel as a test. A trap.

An execution.

"Put me down," she rasped against his jacket, but he

held her tighter, wouldn't let her move. Just kept running. Until they were far enough away. Far enough that no one would find them. Stop him.

"Please," she said, and now she started to struggle. But he was bigger, stronger, and he'd not just come within an inch of meeting his maker to surrender now.

Something had gone wrong. She'd been trapped, too. Maybe the fire started too early—he had no doubt it had been deliberately set. Maybe she'd messed up, had not gotten out in time.

Or maybe Lambert wanted her dead, too.

The thought twisted through John on a violent rush. He glanced around the old houses on either side of the street, saw the overgrown yard beyond the remains of a picket fence. In less than ten strides he was there, kicking open the broken gate and running up the cracked walkway, to the wraparound porch.

He took the three steps in one and rounded the side of the house, didn't stop until he reached the back door. Which again, he kicked open.

Only then did he let himself slow. Think. Breathe.

Only inside did he release his death grip on her and let her move, let her body slide down his and her feet settle against the warped linoleum.

Only then did he take her face in his smoke-scarred hands, and crush her mouth to his.

Chapter 5

His eyes. That's all she saw. In the broken moment before his mouth came down on hers, she saw something steely glowing in his eyes, a neediness that grabbed deep within her, even as her mind shut down. Then she only felt. His mouth slanting against hers. The scrape of whiskers against her cheek. His hands, so big and hard, cradling her face. There was a desperation in his touch, a tenderness that—

A tenderness that made her heart strum low and deep.

It took effort, but she forced herself to pull back, forced herself to open her eyes and look at him. See him. The dirty and torn camouflage pants, the smoke-stained olive T-shirt and field jacket, the solid chest and powerful arms, the hard jaw and the cleft in his chin, the closely cropped dark hair, the impossibly full mouth—the same mouth that had kissed her in her dreams every night for five weeks.

"You," she whispered, then his mouth was on hers again,

and nothing else mattered. She pushed up and lifted her hands, let them touch his face as his touched hers. Beneath her fingers she felt the line of his cheekbone and the warmth of his breath, the softness of his whiskers. And she wanted. She shifted and opened to him, drank him in as greedily as she'd gulped those first few breaths of fresh air.

His body was big and strong and powerful, and in his arms, she felt safe. The horror of the fire faded, the stark realization that she'd made a terrible mistake. There was only the man, and the kiss, and the reality that he'd come for her. He'd emerged from the smoke and—

He'd emerged from the smoke.

Which meant he'd been there. At the old hotel.

Which meant—

In that one cruel instant, everything fractured. She ripped away from him and shoved hard, staggered back.

He made no move to go after her, just remained standing in the shadows of the rickety house and watched with the strangest light in his eyes. "You'll want to breathe—"

"Don't—" Against her raw throat, the word escaped.

"Don't what?" The hoarseness to his voice said he'd inhaled as much smoke as she had. She saw more now that the shadow of life and death had passed, not just his face, but the soot smeared over his cheeks and forehead, the ash on his neck and forearms.

And it hurt. Because when she saw, she remembered. And when she remembered, she felt. And when she felt—

The urge to step closer and wipe it all away had her hands curling into tight fists.

"Don't help you?" he pressed. "Don't tell you how to make it better? Don't touch you? Don't make you remember—"

With a fierceness that came from hidden depths, she angled her chin. "Don't pretend."

"Why not?" He stood so horribly still, all the passion and intensity that had boiled around her moments before congealing into something cold and dangerous. "Isn't that what we do best?"

The words should not have hurt. The words should not have punished. She stood there in her battle stance, refusing to look away, even as she did a quick inventory of her surroundings. The house was abandoned. From the looks of the dilapidated kitchen, had probably stood empty since Katrina. A gas stove remained, but the spot for the refrigerator stood empty. There was no furniture. Nothing to grab as a weapon—except broken glass.

"This was all just a game, wasn't it?" The way he'd touched her. Looked at her. Made her feel. The way he'd wiped away her tears and held her, pressed soft kisses to her forehead. "You were just playing me."

"With you," he corrected with a slow, devastating smile. "We both know games are more fun when played together."

The truth seared through her, bringing not warmth but a penetrating chill she'd not felt since the day she'd dropped a single red rose into a gaping hole in the ground.

"You told him about me." It was the only explanation. The only reason Lambert would want her dead. "You knew he would kill me, but you told him anyway."

The man whose kisses had made her dream again might as well have set the fire himself.

Now he moved. Now he stepped toward her. Just one step, very slow. Very deliberate. "I'm afraid I need you to be a little more specific here, *belle amie*. Told who, what?"

She glanced at the shards of glass beneath the window.

On the sill lay a piece the shape of a flat cola bottle, one edge more jagged than the others. "Is it because I recognized you?" she asked, inching closer. "Because I wasn't useful anymore?" In the distance sirens wailed. "Because you were afraid I would expose you?"

Even as he took another step, the stillness to him deepened. "You don't know when to stop, do you?"

No, she didn't. That had always been one of her greatest strengths—and, according to her brother, an equally great flaw. "You're not going to win," she vowed on a low breath. Lunging, she grabbed the piece of glass and jutted it between them. "Stay where you are."

The lines of his face tightened. "Easy now," he drawled. "You don't want to do that."

Arms extended, she edged toward the back door, which still hung open. "Give me one good reason why not."

"For starters," he said, glancing toward a bulge in his jacket. "I've got a gun."

She took another step. *Never bring a knife to a gunfight* was one of her uncle's favorite sayings—but she didn't have the luxury of choice at the moment. "You going to shoot me?"

He watched her, didn't seem all that concerned. "That wasn't the plan."

If she could get a head start…if she could make it to the busy street one block away. "Back away then," she said.

He moved only slightly, bringing his body against a ledge separating the kitchen from the living area. There, he lounged. "You know you can't go back to him, don't you? Lambert doesn't tolerate failure, not even from pretty ladies."

Failure. It was an odd choice of word. She would have

said *betrayal.* "Then I guess that means you can't go back either," she pointed out.

He shrugged. "Probably not."

Heart kicking hard, she wasted no more time, lunged for the door and started to run. The porch boards protested, but she didn't slow, not even when she tripped on a warped plank. She staggered and caught her balance, raced for the steps.

A few cars lined the sleepy tree-lined street, but none of them moved. She surged out the rusty gate and down the sidewalk, looking for signs of life. Activity. For someone in their yard or a passerby. Her lungs, screaming from the smoke inhalation, burned with every breath, but she ignored the pain. Prytania was only a few blocks away. If she could reach it—

The man rounded the corner on a dead run, and everything blurred. Too late the survivor in her realized her mistake. She hadn't outwitted the stranger. Hadn't outmaneuvered or outrun him. He'd…let her go. He'd let her run from the shadowy kitchen, straight into the path of his accomplice.

Mind racing, she darted across the street and headed between two old houses.

But the new man was faster, and in less than a heartbeat he was on her. They went down hard against the winter-brown grass. The impact crushed her, but she kept fighting, scraping and clawing against the cool, damp ground to crawl out from beneath him.

"Easy now," the man who'd tackled her said—and Saura went very still. That voice. She knew that voice. More than knew it—

On a violent rush she twisted around, and saw. "Cain."

Her brother glared down at her. "Saura? What the hell—"

"Don't hurt her," called another voice, this one equally familiar. "I want her perfectly lucid for what I have in…"

Cain reared back and looked from her to the stranger. His big body tensed, just as it had when she was fifteen and he found her in the foggy back seat of an old Lincoln with an eighteen-year-old. It didn't matter that technically Cain was her little brother. Never had. There'd never been anything "little" about Cain. "*Merde,* D'Ambrosia, do not tell me this is the woman—"

Everything inside of Saura went painfully still. D'Ambrosia. The stranger had a name—and her brother knew it. The heat came next, the realization that if her brother knew D'Ambrosia, and knew about "the woman," then he could know more. A *lot* more.

The stranger she'd given herself to in the bayou, the man she'd played cat and mouse with at the party, who'd dragged her from the burning hotel then kissed her within an inch of her life, stooped down beside them. "There's no mistake."

She saw her brother's eyes darken, knew he was connecting the dots with brutal speed—and consequence. "*She* was the one with Lambert?" It was the dead quiet voice he'd used for interrogations, when he stated dirty ugly facts no one else wanted to repeat.

D'Ambrosia grabbed a red bandanna from a pocket inside his jacket and handed it to her. "You're bleeding." Then to Cain: "Last night."

Her brother barely moved, barely so much as breathed. "In—his—bedroom."

The words, the flat tone, made her cringe. "Cain." She scrambled to her knees. "Just listen, okay. This isn't what you think. I can—"

"Cain?" His mouth a hard line, D'Ambrosia looked

from her brother to her, then back to Cain. "You know this woman?"

Cain grabbed the bandanna and lifted it to her forehead, dabbed at the wound she could neither see nor feel. "You could say so," he bit out. "She's my sister."

The green walls pushed in on John. Two folding chairs sat against the wall, next to a table covered in outdated magazines. The couch that had been here a few months before was gone, the only window nailed shut. Even if he'd been able to pry it open, the bars outside would make it impossible to escape. Not that he needed to escape. Just needed to breathe something other than the stale store-bought disinfectant that permeated the small clinic.

He paced, refused to give in to the urge to push open the door and go down the hall, find out what was taking Cain so long. They'd been in there for forty minutes. Dr. Guidry had been examining a sick baby at the time, but within minutes she'd taken Saura and Cain to one exam room, John into the other. Over his protests her assistant had checked him over. He was fine, just as he'd told them. But Saura—

Christ. Her name twisted low in his gut, even though he did not speak it aloud. *Saura.* Not Lambert's mistress, but Cain's freaking *sister.* A Robichaud. Gabe's cousin. Niece of a United States senator and one of the most powerful sheriffs in the state.

The walls, they pushed a little harder, a hell of a lot closer.

Gabe's urgent message, identifying the woman in the picture as his cousin Saura, had come too late. Shoving a hand through his hair, John strode to the window and stared out at the damp gray day, tried like hell to reconcile everything that had gone down. He and Cain had worked together, but their interactions had never bled into the personal. He'd never been to Cain's house, never met his family. The trip to Bayou de Foi following Alec's death had been his first—

Saura.

Memories slashed through him, of the first night he'd seen her standing across the smoky honky-tonk. She'd worn jeans that night, tight-fitting and a little out of fashion. And a simple black shirt, not silk as he would expect of someone with her kind of money, but a cotton knit. It, too, had looked old, and more than a little big on her.

She'd looked barely put together, as though she'd picked up the outfit at a garage sale in a deliberate attempt to blend into somewhere she categorically did not belong.

But that's not what had gotten him as he'd rolled the warm glass of whiskey between his hands. Her eyes. They'd…haunted him, reminded him of an animal tossed alongside the highway by its owner. Something fierce and raw had glowed in depths he later discovered to be the color of moss, and it had seared through all the indifference and the isolation, blistering him despite the fact he'd long since been beyond the point of feeling. Anything. Except hatred. And loathing. Contempt.

It had not been contempt that he felt. Not even when he'd seen her again on Lambert's arm. That had been excitement, the unholy anticipation of a game he'd neither expected nor wanted, but suddenly looked forward to playing. And winning.

Now… Christ, now she had a name. Saura. And a brother who both trusted and respected him. And she was neither the cat, nor the mouse.

On a low growl he picked up a news magazine and

flipped open the front cover, then threw it across the room. Collette never took this long. She was quick and efficient, and she didn't ask questions. Or file police reports. Which made the lady doctor who split her time between the clinic and Ochsner's popular with those on both sides of the law.

The door shoved open, but it was not Dr. Guidry who strode into the small room, where she stashed those she didn't want anyone else to see. Frowning, Cain closed the door behind him.

John stilled. "What's going on—"

"Collette made me leave the room, said I wasn't doing Saura's blood pressure any good." Frowning, Cain shook his head. "Saura decides to play Nancy Drew and throw herself at a scumbag like Nathan Lambert, and Collette's worried about *her* freaking blood pressure?"

"How high is it?"

Cain blinked. "What?"

"Her blood pressure? How high is it? She inhaled a lot of—"

"She's fine." Her brother bit the words out. "Her lungs are fine. The cut on her forehead is fine." His eyes met John's. "It's her goddamned death wish I'm worried about."

Death wish. It was not a term John liked. "You get anything else out of her? She tell you what she was doing with Lambert?"

Cain grabbed his cell phone and flipped it open, pushed a few buttons then jammed it back in his jeans. "All she'll say is she wants the same thing we do. She and Alec were close. She knows I suspect Lambert, says I should trust her, that she knows what she's doing."

Knows what she's doing. Cozying up to Lambert. Letting the man touch her. Walking into his bedroom. John's gut tightened as the memory of Lambert's big bed flashed into his mind, of Saura alone with that man. In that bed.

He curled his hand into a fist and regrouped, knew he couldn't let emotion twist through his voice. And Holy God in Heaven, he said a grim prayer of thanks he was not a kiss-and-tell kind of man. "Does she have any idea how dangerous Lambert is?"

"You don't know my sister," Cain snapped, and the sudden blast of heat almost made John break out in a sweat. Yanking off his jacket, he tossed it onto a chair and found a sudden interest in the magazines.

He most definitely knew Cain's sister.

"Things like danger and inappropriateness have never stopped her," her brother said. "She used to get off on doing what everyone told her she couldn't, just to prove she could."

John shot Cain a look. "Used to?"

"Up until about two years ago."

"What happened then?" The second he spoke, he made the connection. Two years before Cain Robichaud had been railroaded off the force and out of town. The lynch mob called the media had come dangerously close to picking up the ball the grand jury had dropped.

Saura, apparently, had been caught in the crossfire.

Cain held quiet a long tense moment before answering. The shadows about him, lighter in the months since his lover turned up alive, deepened. "She…" he hesitated "…had a breakdown. It was like she just went away. She was there on the outside, but there was nothing inside. No life. No…anything."

The image formed before John could stop it, and once again he could see her across the bar. The hurt in her eyes. The aching combination of courage and fear. The resolve.

And then, later, after they'd made love, when he'd lifted a hand to her face, and felt tears. He'd looked at her then, their bodies still wrapped together, and had seen a bleakness that would have sent him to his knees, if he'd not been on his back. "And now?"

"That's a damn good question." Cain scowled. "Now I look at her and I see something again. A spark. A…secret. Determination. I noticed it when I got back from Mexico."

The time frame drilled through John. Cain had returned from Mexico five weeks ago…

"But I know my sister," he was saying. "And no matter how hard she pretends, she hasn't healed. Not all the way. She's still broken inside."

John wanted to deny it. All of it. That she wasn't healed. That she was broken inside. That she was hurting—that he'd no doubt made it worse. He looked toward the barred window again and into the light drizzle, but saw only her eyes. As they'd been that night in the bayou. The way they'd sparkled last night, when she'd toyed with him. Then, less than an hour before, the dark glow of passion when she'd pulled back from his kiss and gazed blindly at him. There'd been no masks there in that old kitchen. She'd known who he was. She'd recognized him. She hadn't yet learned Lambert had not sent him to kill her. And still, she'd lifted her mouth to his and pulled him closer, kissed him with the same urgency she had that night in the bayou—

She was broken inside, he reminded himself. And so incredibly off-limits it defied everything he believed in.

Saura dropped a handful of marshmallows into a chipped mug. Ready to indulge, she crossed the breakfast nook and pulled out a chair, sat. Twelve long-stemmed roses dominated the small round table in the plain vase she'd taken from the cabinet upon returning from the apartment several blocks away. Not quite the color of blood, the deep red buds had just started to open. In two days, they would be breathtaking. A day or two beyond that, they would be gone.

If she kept them at all.

Lifting the mug, she enjoyed the feel of the hot liquid sliding against the serrated edges of her throat. She'd taken a long shower with her favorite lavender body wash, but the smell of smoke lingered. Collette said it could be a few days before the vertigo subsided.

Now Saura glanced at the clock, saw the hour pushing deep into the night. Cain had insisted on taking her home, insisted on making sure she was okay. He'd fixed her a sandwich while she cleaned up. He'd paced while she pretended to nap. He'd read her the riot act once he realized she felt fine. He warned her to leave the dirty work to those trained to handle it.

Such as the hard-eyed detective who'd been nowhere in sight when Saura returned to the waiting room.

Silly man. Her brother had no idea how well trained she was. Slipping in and out of the shadows came ridiculously easily to her. Early on she'd learned the benefit of not being taken seriously. Her uncles would talk about things in front of her as if she either wasn't in the room or wasn't capable of understanding what they were saying.

Twenty years had passed since the night her most beloved uncle of all blew his brains out while his children slept upstairs. Saura still recalled the shock of hearing the eyewitness account of her cousin Camille, who insisted two men had been in her father's study. That one of them put the gun to her father's temple—then turned it on her. She'd been found in a wooded area three miles from their house late the next day, wet and cold and suffering from exposure. The authorities had written off her near-incoherent ramblings to grief and imagination.

At first it had puzzled Saura why her family publicly accepted the official ruling of suicide, but privately maintained foul play was involved. Only with time did Saura realize her uncles accepted the lie because something bigger was at play—something she believed was still at play, all these years later. A web, a vendetta, that touched them all.

When she closed her eyes, she could still see Edouard and Etienne chopping wood at the back of the Robichaud property. And she could still hear the name upon which they'd vowed vengeance.

Nathan Lambert.

But the slippery man was still alive, still free, and now Alec was dead. Alec, her friend. Alec, who'd stood beside her when the world turned cold. Alec, who'd figured out her secret, when even her brother had not. Alec, who'd contacted her during the final days of his life, asking what she knew about Nathan Lambert. What she could find out.

Alec, whom she would not let down.

Frowning, she set down her mug and picked up her cordless phone, listened to her messages for the third time in the hour since Cain had finally left her alone.

"It wasn't the same after you left last night," Lambert said in a sleep-heavy voice. At the time he'd left the message, she'd been en route to the old hotel. "Please let me know you're okay. I worry about you."

"It's after lunch, Dawn." That was the name she'd given him, the identity she'd created. A woman from a small

Mississippi town, in New Orleans to satisfy a taste for adventure. "Call me a foolish old man, but I need to know that you're okay." A fishing expedition, she wondered? A way of determining if she'd perished in the fire? "Please. Call me back."

The final message was brilliant for its simplicity: "Call me back, sweetheart. I'm worried."

She hadn't called him back. At least not yet. Not until she retrieved the tapes from the surveillance equipment she'd stashed in his neighbor's yard and determined if she was the one who'd been targeted to perish in the fire.

She'd never been caught before. Never really come close. She wasn't a woman to make mistakes. That was her M.O., why demand for her services had once far surpassed supply. She operated with care and precision. She could extract what she wanted and no one would be the wiser. She never left tracks.

She never got caught.

But that was before, she realized, fingering the card that had come with the roses. *True beauty,* it read, *knows no rival.*

A ridiculously romantic gesture? Or a moderately clever cover-up? What man, after all, sent roses to a woman on the day he meant to execute her?

Nathan Lambert, she recalled, had played poker with her uncle Troy less than twenty-four hours before his so-called suicide. He'd gone to the funeral. And...he'd sent flowers.

True determination, she thought with one last sip of now lukewarm chocolate, knew no limits.

Standing, Saura turned out the light and headed for her bedroom. No matter how much she wanted to crawl into bed, she had tapes to retrieve.

She had two buttons unfastened when the sound of a fist

on wood jolted through the old house. She stood so very still, listening. Waiting. Cain had a key—and as far as she knew, no one else knew where she lived. And no one else had reason to visit during the dead of night.

Another knock. Louder. More forceful.

Instinct and training swirled through her in a rush, and without even thinking about what she was doing, she moved away from the window and pressed her back to the wall, eased toward the dresser that had once belonged to her grandmother. From inside her pajama drawer—the lingerie drawer was much too obvious—she retrieved the new Kahr 9mm she'd purchased after her night with D'Ambrosia. The newest innovation, the gun shop owner had told her. Light-weight and compact, easily concealed and highly accurate.

From afternoons spent at the shooting range, she knew he'd spoken the truth.

Slipping barefoot into the hallway, she told herself she was overreacting. It was probably just a neighbor. Or someone looking for a lost dog. At midnight.

The urgent pounding killed both theories. Her late-night visitor was not here for a social call. And they weren't going away. If she did not answer, they would come in anyway. That was the purpose of the pounding. A test, much like the phone calls and the flowers. To see if she would open the door willingly. Or—

The memory slammed her from somewhere broken, and before she could even breathe Cain was there again, bruising his hand against the door of Adrian's condo. In the middle of the night. She'd pulled herself from bed and staggered to the door, not stopping to realize that if her fiancé had locked himself out, he would not be banging against the door as if his life depended on it.

She'd been three feet away when the door flew open, and Cain charged in. She'd never seen him like that, so pale and shaken. It was only later that she'd learned why, that he'd stormed the condo like a commando on a suicide mission because he thought someone had gotten to her, too.

That someone had eliminated her just as they'd done Adrian. With a bullet through the heart.

Shoving aside the images, she lifted the gun and curled her finger around the trigger.

This time, she would not go down without a fight.

Chapter 6

John pulled his hand from the door and took two steps back, caught himself in the boiling moment before he kicked.

He was a cop, damn it. He knew how to stay calm when the world exploded around him. He knew the unexpected beauty of patience. How to use it. Milk it. He'd learned the importance of staying in control. Of never letting emotion slip in. Never letting it bleed through.

Never letting it so much as form.

Standing in the shadow of the old porch, without even a sliver of moonlight to guide him, he reached for his Glock and released the lock, but did not slide his finger around the trigger. Protocol guided his actions—or at least it was supposed to. Sometimes it was instinct that drove him. Instinct that kept him alive while others died.

Instinct that kept him on the porch, when common sense told him to walk away—and something even more dangerous told him to gain access by whatever means necessary.

The memory slashed, another day. Another closed door. Alec walking toward it. John running, shouting for his friend to stop. Alec reaching for the handle. Alec pulling.

The world exploding.

Narrowing his eyes against the horrific aftermath, John ripped his gaze from the door and stepped toward the glow from the small window. She was in there. In bed, he told himself. Exhausted. Cain had been with her until a short time before. John had been watching ever since. No one had come to her door. She was safe. Lambert had not come to finish what he'd started.

Unless he'd come through the rear.

On a violent rush, John pressed his back to the siding and eased next to the window, moved his finger to the trigger and looked inside. And saw her.

She stood beyond the living room, in a narrow hallway with her back to the wall, much as his was. Dark hair fell against her face. Oversize pajamas hung from her shoulders. And in her hand, she held what looked like a 9mm.

The sight of her, of the horrible tangle of uncertainty and courage in her gaze, punched through John like a fist to the gut.

He'd done this to her. He'd meant to protect, but by banging on her door in the middle of the night, he'd sent her into a nightmare he'd never intended.

"Saura." His voice. She needed his voice, no matter how smoke-roughened it was. To know that it was him who stood outside. Not someone who wanted to hurt her. "It's me. D'Ambrosia."

She didn't move, didn't blink. He wasn't sure she breathed.

"Belle amie." He wasn't a man to use endearments, but damn it, in that moment, it felt right. "I'm not going to hurt you."

No matter how hard she pretends otherwise, Cain had said, *she's still broken inside.*

"You can trust me," he added, and the words scraped. "I just want to—" *See you. Make sure you're okay. Make sure you stay away from Lambert. That he never has the chance to touch you again. To hurt you. To break you.*

Chest tight, John crushed the ridiculous internal dialogue and focused on the one promise he could make. "Talk."

Through the shadows, he saw something hard and ragged flicker through her expression.

"Tell me what to do." He kept his voice low, calm, much like he used with victims of domestic violence. *Tell me where it hurts.* "Tell me what you need."

Finally she moved. With the gun still held in front of her, she lifted her free hand to shove the hair from her face and stepped forward, kept her movements slow, measured. In control.

Because of her family, he told himself. She'd grown up a Robichaud, an impressionable young girl among a family of powerful men. It made sense that she would have learned and absorbed, becoming more dangerous with each day that passed.

He wondered if her family realized.

Somehow he doubted that they did.

"Step away from the window and put down your gun," she called, and he smiled. He also obeyed, shifted to the old rail.

"Done," he told her, hating the fact that he could no longer see her, not even her silhouette against the window.

But she was moving into position to look at him, he knew. So for effect, he lifted his hands.

Light then, bright and glaring, exposing him standing next to a thirsty fern like a suspect in a lineup. "Just me. No one else."

Slowly, the door opened. Light glowed through a narrow crack, revealing a chain, but not her. "What do you want?"

"I told you," he said. "To talk."

"It's after midnight."

"Your brother was here. I didn't think you'd want an audience."

Silence then. For just a moment. Then the door closed and the chain jingled, and there she was, standing in the open doorway.

Flannel. The knowledge twisted through him. The too-big pajamas were off-white, with a parade of penguins scattered about. In them, with her hair tangled around her face and her eyes huge and dark, she looked about seventeen years old.

And goddamn it, he wanted to kiss her anyway. Kiss her hard. Pull her into his arms and put his mouth to hers, pick up where they'd left off that morning in the kitchen.

"You can put down your gun," he said instead.

Her chin came up. "You realize I don't want you here, don't you?"

It took effort, but he bit back the dark laughter. "I kind of noticed that."

"Did Cain send you?"

"Would that make you feel better if he did?"

Her eyes flared in the brief instant before she glanced toward the quiet street behind him. Left, then right. Left again.

She was good, he couldn't help but think. Thorough. Disturbingly cautious. No one behaved that way without reason.

"Get in," she said, returning her gaze to his.

The contrast between the point-blank words and the cuddly pajamas tightened through him. "Would you like to pick that up?" He gestured toward his gun. "Or shall I?"

Never taking her eyes from his, never changing the aim of her 9mm, she squatted and retrieved his semiautomatic, then straightened and motioned him inside.

More disturbed by the second, he kept his eyes on hers and moved slowly toward the open door. She backed away when he almost touched, closed the door as soon as he crossed the threshold. Never releasing him from her gaze, she turned the bolt but did not fasten the chain—he didn't want to wonder why. But did.

She looked at him as if she didn't have a clue who he was. As if she'd never watched him from across a smoky bar. Never approached him. Never let him touch her. Never lifted her mouth to his. Never cried in his arms.

Never held on as though she couldn't let go.

"You know I'm a cop, right?" Vanilla. The scent whispered around him, bringing with it the faintest trace of roses. "A detective. One of the good guys."

She fought it, but he would have sworn he saw her mouth twitch. Her lips were pale, slightly cracked. "I know you have a badge and a gun," she said, and though the words were hard, the tangle of dark hair against her make-upless face gave them a softness he knew she would hate. The bottle of pale-pink nail polish sitting on the table by the door didn't help. "But that doesn't make you one of the good guys."

He let out a rough breath. "You think I'm dirty?" The question came out harsher than he'd intended. "I saved your life, damn it," he growled, and this time he moved, despite the guns. He destroyed the distance between them and put his hand to the butt of the 9mm, turned it away. "You really think that's the action of a man on Lambert's payroll?"

Her eyes went dark. "If that man wants to gain my trust and make me think he's on my side—yes. If he wants to use me—yes. If he likes to toy with people, to play with people—"

"No." He took her shoulders and pulled her close, lifted a hand to slide the hair from her face. Her eyes, damn it. He wanted to see them—needed to see them. And God almighty, even more he needed *her* to see *him*. "What happened to you?" he asked, as the shadow of Cain's words fell around them. "Who did this to you?"

For a long moment she said nothing. Just looked up at him with her chin at a fierce angle, her mouth a mutinous line.

John wasn't sure he'd ever wanted to kiss a woman more.

"Just because a woman doesn't take chances," she finally said, "doesn't mean something has happened to her."

In other words, she wasn't about to tell him. *"Touché."* But he wasn't about to let her shimmy away that easily. "But I'm not talking about *not* taking chances." He paused, could feel the jerky rise and fall of her shoulders beneath his hands. "I was there," he reminded, making it explicitly clear he'd seen everything she tried to hide. Everything she wanted to deny. "At Lucky's," he clarified, when she'd tempted him with an honesty he wasn't sure he'd ever experienced. "Last night." When she'd put her arms around him and pretended he was a stranger, even as her body clearly remembered every detail of the last time they'd been together. "This morning." When she'd pulled back from his kiss and blinked at him, only to tug him back for more. "No matter what you have or have not told your brother, I saw everything. And I know you're not afraid of taking chances."

He wasn't certain what he expected, but it sure as hell was not for her to push up on her toes and lift a hand to his face, tap a finger against his lower lip. "Calculated risks," she said with a slow, take-no-prisoners smile. "There is a difference."

Everything inside of him went very still. Because of what he'd seen, he told himself. Because of what he knew. Not because of the words she'd just spoken. Not because he knew they could only lead to one place.

"Tell that to Alec." For the first time since he'd seen her standing with the gun in her hand, the kid gloves came off. Gentleness had its place. But so did toughness. "He took a calculated risk and look where it got him—"

Her eyes narrowed. "You were there, weren't you?" Through the shadows of her living room she stared at him as if he wasn't a man but a window. And through him she could see something that horrified her. "The day he died."

John wasn't a man to look away first. He wasn't a man to yield. But he couldn't just stand there and let her pick apart his memories. Couldn't let her see what he'd seen. Hear what he'd heard. *Feel what he'd felt.*

"You were the one who tried to stop him." There was a dawning awareness in her quiet voice, as if she were connecting dots with lines she'd not recognized before. "Gabe told me— You knew it was a setup and—"

He stopped her. "Put the gun down, Saura."

For a moment she looked confused. Then she glanced at her hand, still clenched around the butt of the 9mm. And much to his surprise, she set it on the old secretary just behind her.

"You were at his funeral," she whispered. "I saw you—"

"I was his partner," he said. In his mind, that explained all of his actions regarding Alec.

"But no one else from the force was there." She kept on, and damn it, he didn't need to be a detective to realize the tide had just shifted into an unwanted direction. "*Just you.* Because you knew he wasn't dirty. You knew turning in his badge was part of some elaborate game—"

He reached for her so fast he had no time to think. No time to retreat. He took her shoulders and pulled her close, felt her legs bump against his. "Not a game, *cher.* None of this." Something hard and dark splintered through him, shredding everything it touched. "Nathan Lambert is a dangerous man. He killed Alec because he got too close, and he'll kill you, too—"

Dark hair slipped against her face. "I'm well aware of that."

"I don't think you are." He ignored the punishing softness to her voice, the even more punishing softness of her body. "What do you think he'll do when he realizes there was no body in the hotel? That you weren't there? That you slipped away—"

"He'll come after me." She spoke with a matter-of-factness that fired his blood, as if she wasn't the least bit concerned about the thought of Nathan Lambert coming after her.

…it's her death wish I'm worried about.

John ignored the scrape of Cain's words and forced himself to hear what she was saying. "…that is, if the fire really was meant for me."

He felt the lines of his face go tight. "That fire was no accident."

"I'm well aware of that," she said, still looking up at him as if they were discussing the pros and cons of adding okra to gumbo. "But it's possible I was simply at the wrong place at the wrong time."

He wasn't sure which alarmed him more—that she might actually believe what she said. Or that she could be right. "That's not a chance I'm willing to take."

"That *you're* not willing to take?" Finally some emotion bled into her voice. "Is that why you came banging on my door in the middle of the night, Detective?" It was the first time she'd referred to him as anything other than *étranger.* Stranger. "To scurry me into hiding or send me into protective custody?" Against his hands she squirmed, but he refused to let her go. "Or maybe you're just here to try and scare me—"

"Damn it, Saura," he growled, grabbing for the tattered remains of a control some called legendary—but the strobe light of images blasted harder. Faster. Darker. Of Saura. And Lambert. Alone. No one to stop him—no one to hear her last breath. "You should be afraid."

The dangerously quiet words whispered through Saura. The chill started low and spread fast, feathered out to touch her in ways she didn't want to be touched. In places that had been disturbingly warm only seconds before. Places that immediately went cold.

She wanted to be angry at him. She wanted to rip out of his arms and pull open the door. Send him on his way. Never cross his path again. But the scorched-earth look in his eyes made it impossible for her to look away.

This man…she no more understood him than she understood the quickening moving through her, the urge to lift a hand to his face and touch, to skim her fingers along the dark whiskers of his jaw, to the softness of his lower lip.

"Tell me something." She refused to allow herself to relent. Not for so much as one heartbeat. "Are *you* scared?" Some would call the edge to her voice a taunt. "Is that what this is about? Is that why you're here?"

He didn't move, his hands curled around her shoulders, his grip firm but with the same gentleness he always showed her. Like the good cop she now knew him to be, he gave no sign that her question had hit its target. Except for the deepening of the cleft in his chin.

Saura tried not to feel the thrill, but the memory intruded anyway—the night in the cabin, when she'd lifted first her finger to his chin. Then her mouth. Then, finally, her tongue.

"You have no idea what scares me," he said in a dead quiet voice that sent her heart on a long, slow free fall.

She kept her chin angled, refused to let him see the intense curiosity swirling deeper. She'd called him *étranger* in the bayou, but the joke had been on her. Their paths had never directly crossed, but she could have filled several newspapers with what she knew about the man. She could have kept a blog running for months. She'd heard the stories, after all. From Cain. And Gabe. And Alec. And even when she'd felt nothing, she'd found herself asking questions. Wanting to know more.

Because even as a stranger, the man had fascinated.

During the time when her brother had lost both his faith and trust in law enforcement, D'Ambrosia had been one of the few to stand by him. To risk his own career to help clear Cain's name. Her brother more than respected this man. He trusted him.

Saura looked up at him now, through the shadows of her small house, but did not see the man of singular focus her brother had told her about, the one who neither took prisoners nor made compromises. Who routinely requested assignments no one else wanted. Who could rub elbows with the criminal elite as easily as he could blend with the burgeoning drug subculture. Who'd stayed on duty after Katrina, when so many of his fellow officers had fled. Who'd gone through house after house…

Who walked away at the end of his shift without turning back.

Nor did she see the man who drove himself and tested himself, who could empty round after round into a target while a bandanna covered his eyes. Who never joined his colleagues for a beer. Whose desk had no pictures of loved ones.

Who allegedly saw everything, and felt nothing.

Saura wanted to see that man. She wanted to see the emptiness. The soulless eyes. But it was the man from Lucky's who stood so close she couldn't breathe without pulling the scent of soap and leather and him deep within her. It was the man from the cabin, who'd touched her and held her.

And though rumor had it nothing scared Detective John D'Ambrosia, the primal glitter in his eyes made her wonder. "Then tell me," she whispered.

He did nothing at first. Didn't speak. Didn't move. She didn't even think he breathed. But then he lifted a hand from her and skimmed it along her neck, brought it to the side of her face. She shivered. Five weeks before, as she'd stood naked in the darkness, he'd pulled her against him as he unfastened her French braid. Then, he'd run his fingers through her hair and let it fall against her shoulders. Now he lifted a single finger, and twirled a single strand.

"The call comes in the middle of the night," he said in a disturbingly emotionless voice. "I answer on the first ring. Six minutes later I'm out the door. Twenty-two minutes later, I get out of my car and walk past the poor schmuck who found the body."

Saura stilled. She ignored the feel of his finger tangled in her hair and absorbed him, not the stranger from the bayou as he'd been moments before, but the driven detective her brother had told her about. His eyes had gone flat, leaving only the objective cop, walking through the night to a crime scene.

Police work changed people, she knew. Forced them to compartmentalize their lives. Good versus bad. Work versus home. But that was impossible, she also knew. Stains had a way of spreading one fiber at a time, corroding whatever they touched.

"He's been on the force for years," he was saying, his voice a monotone. "He's a good cop. Thorough. Desensitized. But now he's pale and his eyes are glassy, and from the smell I know he's just lost his dinner."

The slippery sense of dread stunned her. She'd asked the question. She'd wanted to know what scared him. But she hadn't really expected an answer, had been throwing down a dare rather than voicing a genuine curiosity.

Now he wouldn't stop touching, wouldn't stop twirling her hair around his finger, watching her with a detached intensity that made her wish she'd taken the time to pull on the biggest, thickest robe she owned...

"But I keep walking," he went on, and even though she had no idea where he was going, she was there with him. Moving through the night. "I've seen the coroner's car. I know he's inside. So are the paramedics. But they're just standing a few feet from the door. They're not needed anymore."

But John was. A detective, John had to face what no one else wanted to see. He had to see, and touch, and understand. To envision those last final moments and put together bloodstained pieces that lay fractured beyond recognition.

"It's dark." But Saura already knew that. She could see the stillness of the night. Felt it radiating from the man whose thighs brushed her own. "There's not much light inside, just one lamp in the corner. The CSI photographer is squatting near the body. Each flash of his camera reveals the blood on the floor." He hesitated, shifting his hair-wrapped finger to stroke the underside of her jaw. "The walls."

Outside the wind whispered against the windows. Inside, the heater spewed warm air from vents along the wood floor. But the coldness moved through Saura like ice laying siege to a stream.

"Then I see the sheriff," John added, but now she wanted him to stop. She didn't want to see what he saw. Know what he knew. "He's a grizzled old man. Fought in 'Nam." Hesitating, he let silence spill between them. But he never released her from his gaze. "Some call him the Silver Fox."

Everything closed in on Saura—the dark blue walls of the old house, the heat of John's body swirling around hers—and the name. The Silver Fox. Her uncle.

"He's crying." John bit out the words, and now his face changed. The glitter returned to his eyes, the recrimination to his voice. His forefinger remained against her jaw, but now his thumb joined it in a slow dance. "Leaning over his nephew."

Her brother, Cain.

"Who," John added, "is on his knees, next to his sister's body."

Saura ripped away from him, and tried to breathe. "John, don't—"

"So it's John now?" He lounged against the old secretary like a cop one hundred percent in control. "Because it sure wasn't that night, was it?" The cleft in his chin deepened. "It was *étranger,* wasn't it? Stranger."

She backed away, couldn't believe she hadn't seen the trap he'd so methodically laid. She'd asked the question; she'd wanted to know. What scared a man like Detective John D'Ambrosia?

But she'd never expected him to throw the night they'd made love back into her face, to twist those mindless hours into something dark and horrific. To paint in very explicit terms what could happen to a woman who went home with the wrong man.

"You left that bar with me, anyway, didn't you?" he pressed with a ruthlessness she recognized too well. "You didn't tell anyone where you were going—you didn't *know* where you were going."

The truth of his words stabbed through her.

"But you went anyway," he said, and now his lips curved into a slow, languorous smile. "To have sex with me."

He made it sound so crass and dirty, so…calculated.

So stupid.

"Don't look so shocked, sugar. It's no secret, at least not between us." Nor was the way his gaze slipped from her face to the pajama top that hung open at her chest. "I was there. I saw the way you looked at me. I felt the way you touched me."

And she'd felt the way he'd touched her. So softly. So gently. With a need that had scorched clear down to her soul.

"Get out." She refused to let him stand there so smug and superior, acting as though she was a foolish twit so hot for him that she'd thrown caution to the wind. "Take your stupid games and get the hell—"

"You were scared," he said as she whirled toward him, "but that didn't stop you from leaving with me. You knew what you were doing was reckless, but that didn't stop you, either."

She narrowed her eyes. "Maybe I didn't care—"

"Bingo." He covered the distance between them before she could so much as breathe. "You didn't care," he said, closing in on her. "Nathan Lambert doesn't care. You see something you want, you go after it. You take it. And if someone gets hurt in the process, you don't care."

Her heart kicked hard. "You're twisting my words—"

Eyes on fire, he backed her against the doorjamb. "I could have killed you," he said, lifting a hand to her throat. "So many times." His callused fingers feathered against her neck. "In so many ways." His thumb dipped into the V of her collarbone. "You were at my mercy," he said, and his expression darkened. "I could have done anything—and no one would have been there to stop me."

She swallowed hard, refused to give him the satisfaction of defending herself. Of explaining.

"But you got naked with me anyway," he added in a dead quiet voice that made her throat go tight. "You lifted your mouth to mine and took what I had to give." Slowly, he slid his pinkie along to her bottom lip. "Then you took more."

Then she'd walked away.

With his body sandwiching her against the door, Saura knew she should get away from him. Shove him onto his back and slam the door in his face. And yet, against the silence she heard what he did not say, saw what he did not want her to see. And perhaps most damning of all, felt what he did not want her to feel. The restraint, and the fear.

His eyes held the same bone-chilling dread she'd seen when he'd insisted she had no idea what scared him.

But now she did know, and the knowledge disturbed as much as it thrilled. Detective John D'Ambrosia, this man who allegedly felt nothing, felt everything. Deeply. It wasn't machismo or ego that drove him, wasn't a deep need for control that led him to try to dismantle her investigation. It was…fear. For her. Because of the night in the bayou, when a leap of faith had propelled her into taking the biggest chance of her life.

She knew she should say something—refute or deny or defend—but there was nothing to say. Because he was right. As much as she hated to admit it, he was right. He could have killed her. Easily. Brutally. She would have put up a fight, but he was bigger, stronger, and in the end, he would have won. But she'd left with him anyway. She'd gotten naked. She'd given herself to a man who could have taken so much more.

Who *had* taken—

She blocked the thought before it could form, refused to feel one blade of empathy or admiration for this man who could crush the future she was beginning to realize she wanted.

"So tell me," he said, shattering the silence. "Is that what you're going to do with Lambert? Get him alone in that big bedroom. Look at him in that way of yours," he added, reaching for her hand and curling his fingers around her palm, skimming his thumb along the sensitive flesh there. "Touch him and get him all hot and bothered—"

Because the image he painted disgusted her, she lifted her chin and let a slow smile curve her lips. "It worked with you, didn't it?"

Chapter 7

The moon had come out. Earlier, when he'd charged her front porch, there'd been only darkness. Now the goddamn moon glowed through the naked branches and flirted with her face, revealing the defiance in her eyes. Her body vibrated with challenge—a fact his noticed too well. He could feel all of her, the curves and the softness and the heat, the jerky rise and fall of her shoulders. No matter how unaffected she pretended to be, by his words, his presence, the frenetic riff of her heart gave her away.

Because in that moment, there was nothing cold, or still.

Stepping closer, he allowed his hips to rock against hers, allowed her to feel the hard lines of his body. But he did not allow himself to touch her as he wanted. And he did not allow himself to take her face in his hands, and lower his mouth to hers. To taste and—

"You think you know what you're doing," he said,

reaching for her hand and closing his fingers around her palm. The warmth of her flesh defied the untouchable facade she was trying to portray. "So maybe you sidestep him the first time," he added, drawing their hands to the door beside her face. "Maybe you have a headache." Just the thought of her alone with that man sickened him. "But you don't know when to stop, and neither does he. So the next time you're together, he's got insurance."

Pressed up against his, her body tensed.

"Maybe he knows what you're really after. Maybe he doesn't. But it doesn't matter—*because he doesn't care.* He just wants what he wants."

Her eyes went dark, and before she even spoke, he knew he was finally hitting a nerve. "Kind of like you, *étranger?*"

The urge to grin surprised him. "Maybe you'll get a chance to tell him no. Or maybe he'll make you beg." The words scraped on the way out. "For your life—or for more. He can do that, you know." Curled inside of his, her hand chilled.

It was all he could do not to rub.

"It only takes one little drink, laced with rohypnol, GHB, or any other roofie," he forced himself to say.

Her mouth opened slightly, and from her expression he knew she recognized the names of the most common date rape drugs.

"Two little milligrams and he'll have you on your back and eager for—"

She shoved him, hard, and even though he could have held her in place, he let her put distance between them. "Is that what scares you?" she asked with a sugary calm that fascinated. "Me? With Nathan?"

The sound of Lambert's first name on her tongue made his blood pump hot and hard. "You asked the question, *belle amie.* I'm just giving it to you straight." As he'd done his entire police career. But never before had the truth boiled like acid in his gut. "I've seen what men like Lambert do. The carnage in their wake. If you want to vilify me for trying to make sure you're not another casualty, go ahead. But know this. I'll be watching." Because she was his friend's sister, he told himself. Because she was innocent in all this.

But even as he spoke, he recognized the lie. "If you so much as breathe the same air that man does, I'll know."

Her smile was slow and amused and damn near made him come unglued. "I'll keep that in mind."

In other words, she was going to damn well do as she pleased.

Because he didn't trust himself to be around her one second longer, not without doing something they'd both regret, he turned to leave. But a blur of red caught his eye. He spun toward the interior of the ridiculously cozy house, where through a pass-through he saw a small round table. With roses on top.

And he knew. God Christ almighty, before he even took the first step, he knew.

"What are you doing?" Saura demanded, finally, finally sounding off balance. But he was already across the living room and into the kitchen, grabbing the green glass vase. He took it to the sink and shook the long stems out, letting all twelve buds tumble against stainless steel.

"John—"

He grabbed the card, read the message, felt everything inside him go stone cold. On a hard breath he turned and found her standing too close, just barely prevented a collision.

He so did not trust himself to touch her right now.

She stood there in her flannel pajamas, with her hair spilling around her face and a question in her eyes. Beyond her, on the counter, sat a fat cat cookie jar. There was an old-fashioned teakettle on the gas stove.

"He knows where you live?" The question tore out of him. He looked back at her and tried like hell not to see the woman who lived in this house, the woman who displayed faded photographs and had a tattered afghan on her sofa, who put marshmallows in her hot chocolate.

Her eyes met his. "I don't owe you any explanations, you know."

The words were tart. Her voice was…not. He ignored both. "Do you have any idea—"

"Yes." Snatching the card, she crumpled it in hers. "I know what would happen if Nathan knew where I lived." Frowning, she opened the cabinet beneath the sink and tossed the wadded card into the trashcan. "Do you really think I'm that careless? That I would have pictures of my family—*my brother, for God's sake*—lying around, if there was even a sliver of a chance Lambert might see them?"

Yes. The word boiled through him. She was a woman who believed there was a difference between chances and calculated risks. In the five short weeks he'd known her, he could think of at least three times she'd taken her life into her own hands. Without a safety net.

But here in her kitchen, he didn't see the daredevil. He saw the woman. Cain's sister and Gabe's cousin. A Robichaud. In her eyes glowed the same fierce intelligence he'd seen from others in her family on too many occasions to count. The same cunning. But there was a gentleness there, too, something soft and protective and…wounded. And it painted a far different picture than he wanted to see.

Which, in turn, made her far, far more dangerous

Yes, she was reckless. Yes, she took risks. And yes, she would gamble with her life. But not with her family. She would never jeopardize them. Like every other Robichaud, she would lay down her life to protect those she loved—

The thought stopped him cold. Protect. Those. She. Loved.

Saura was trying to protect someone—someone she loved. And she was willing to risk her life to do it.

"Then how did the roses get here?" he asked.

The smile surprised him. It was sad and faint, and damn near knocked the breath from his lungs. "I brought them," she said, and he couldn't help but think this was the real Saura talking, without defense mechanisms and shields of bravado, without pretense or ammunition. "Thought it'd be a shame for them to die alone."

His smile surprised him even more. It was equally faint, but he refused to let it be anything else. "You brought them."

"I keep an apartment in an old brownstone in the warehouse district," she said, reaching for the vase and refilling it with water. Then she replaced the roses. Artfully. "That's where he picks me up and drops me off."

John watched her slender fingers toy with the long stems, how they handled the thorns without missing a beat. "He's been inside?"

He hated the way the question burned on the way out.

"Of course." She reached for the last rose. "It's fully furnished, with clothes and food, pictures and magazines and—"

"A bed?"

In the sink her hands stilled. Through the hair falling into her face she looked up at him, with an odd combination of surprise and hesitation in the dark moss of her eyes. "He thinks I live there," she said quietly. "Without a bed, don't you think Nathan might get a bit suspicious?"

Nathan. Not Lambert.

Taking the rose from her hand, he ignored the sharp stab and shoved the stem into the vase. "Most men would," he agreed, wiping the smear of blood on his fingertip against his jeans.

"The sheets are wrinkled." She took his hand and turned on the water, moving his finger under the stream. "Even though the bed has never been slept in."

He pulled his hand back, knew he had to get the hell out of there. "If you want to stay alive, you'll keep it that way." Frowning, he turned and headed toward the door.

"John—"

Not *étranger*. Not Detective.

From the threshold he turned back and forced himself to ignore the way she looked standing by the antique secretary, with those liquid eyes trained on him. The porch light brightened the area, illuminating an old black-and-white photo—one featuring younger versions of Cain and Gabe and an unknown girl—through the glass doors. Its position—prominent yet protected—in her home made him wonder.

He bit back the thought, knew better than to wonder. Not about the woman who pretended to be a daredevil, not about the flicker of vulnerability she didn't want anyone to see.

"There's something you should know," he said. "Nathan Lambert isn't the only man who knows how to get what he wants."

Then he walked into the night.

* * *

She gave him fifteen minutes. During that time she slipped into jeans and a turtleneck, braided her hair and pulled on a knit cap. With a check of the clock above the stove, she flipped out the light and double-checked the locks, then returned to her bedroom. There, Saura fired up her laptop and checked e-mail.

After deleting a fresh batch of spam, she powered down and went into her closet, checked the closed-circuit monitor that maintained a vigil on the perimeter. No one, not Nathan Lambert nor Detective D'Ambrosia, was going to catch her by surprise.

Once she was sure no one lurked outside, she grabbed her purse and let herself into the alley, walked the length of four houses before exiting on the street behind her.

In thirty minutes she would arrive at the house adjacent to Lambert's St. Charles Avenue mansion. There, tucked securely in his neighbor's overgrown bougainvillea, she had a tape to retrieve, and one very important question to answer.

"This her?"

John glanced at the fuzzy pictures he'd taken with his cell phone camera, of Saura with the wrong color hair—and the wrong man. "Normally she's a brunette," he said, sliding a second series of pictures onto the sticky table at the back of The Easy Note. He'd been surprised how few hits he'd encountered when he'd done an Internet search on Saura Robichaud. With her family, he'd expected her picture to be splashed across any number of Web sites.

It wasn't.

"These are a few years old," he said, lining up the shots of Saura with a succession of men—her uncle the senator at a campaign event, her brother and cousin at what looked to be a graduation celebration, and finally, a third picture with a fourth man. Adrian Doucet. Her fiancé, according to the news story. Who'd been murdered in cold blood two years ago.

There'd been no pictures, no mentions, of Saura Robichaud since then.

T'Paul Lareau stubbed out his cigarette and picked up the picture of Saura with Cain and Gabe. Narrowing his eyes, he put it back on the table, and used his fingers to block out everything but the oval of Saura's face. "She ever go blond?"

"Probably." Watching his trusted, but very-under-the-radar informant, John saw something in the other man's eyes he categorically did not like. "You know her?"

T'Paul reached for the picture of Saura and her fiancé. "Thought so," he drawled, reaching for a new cigarette. "But maybe not. The woman I'm thinking of is supposed to be dead."

"How long?" John asked.

"Two, maybe three years."

The time frame fit. "What was her name? How'd you know her?"

"Didn't really know her," the informant said. "Just saw her around the Quarter and at the track. At Jazz Fest one year." He slid his unlit cigarette along the photo of Saura and her uncle. "But the broad I'm thinking of never dressed like this," he said, outlining her simple, slim-fitting rose-colored gown. "Black was more her color. And her hair was usually blond. Sometimes red."

The blade of unease John had been fighting from the moment he'd learned her identity drove deeper. A socialite going single-handedly after a notorious criminal…something so didn't add up. "And you thought she was dead?"

"Everyone did."

"Who's everyone?"

T'Paul ripped a match from the book and dragged it along the inside strip. "No one in particular, it's just no one saw her anymore. She just—vanished, like some of those casino owners who ticked off the Russian Mafia. I figured a pretty thing like her must've gotten mixed up with something she shouldn't have."

Or some*one*.

John reached for the pictures he'd taken of Saura and Lambert, resisted the urge to fold them in his hands. "Might be her," he conceded, trying to fit the pieces together.

Saura Robichaud was a woman of secrets. She was clever and she was guarded. But she was also…vulnerable. It wasn't a word he liked—and he knew damn sure it wasn't a label she would appreciate. But he couldn't shake the memory of her in those ridiculous pajamas.

"Here's what I need you to do. Follow her. Find out where she goes. Who she sees. How long she stays." He paused as the waitress delivered his beer, slid her a five, then picked up the bottle and took a long sip. "She's got an apartment in the warehouse district." He set the bottle onto the table. "Find it."

Saura slipped her hand into the pocket of her bulky jacket and closed her fingers around the small tape recorder. She'd retrieved it with ease, had returned to her house less than ninety minutes after slipping down the alley. She'd entered the same way she exited, then slipped through the darkness to her closet, where the closed-circuit monitor had revealed a man slumped against the iron fence of a vacant house across the street. A vagrant, perhaps.

But she didn't think so.

Now she lifted her face to the cool morning breeze, knew her brother, a nature photographer, would appreciate the way the sun glinted against the watery carpet of duckweed. Along the shores of the no-name lake, frail-looking cypress trees jutted up against the gray sky, providing shelter for a handful of egrets. Winter had stripped the oak and maples of their leaves, but along their naked branches clusters of buds waited for the temperature to warm.

Following the narrow path, she was careful to keep her feet from crunching down on twigs or leaves. A heaviness hung in the air, something between mist and fog. She'd dressed accordingly, braiding hair with a tendency to curl into a long strip down her back.

From the moment she'd heard the audiotape she'd retrieved in the quiet of predawn, she'd known what she had to do. Now as she skirted around the rotting carcass of a fallen tree, she knew she was close. Around her the silence deepened, creating a stillness that should signify she was alone. But she knew she was not.

To her right, a heron called to its mate. Or maybe that was an egret. Cain would know, but Saura wasn't sure. Didn't care, either.

Beyond a single weeping willow, an old wood structure sat recessed from the main path. She headed toward it, but rather than going for the door, she slipped next to the darkened window and looked inside. A table, a soda can, a book and a laptop computer. That was all.

Her heart kicked hard, but she did not go inside. Instead

she followed a walkway to the rear of the fishing shack—and through the narrow streams of sunlight saw him.

He stood on the edge of what once had been a pier, two rotting boards jutting out like a diving board over the cold water of the lake. He wore only a pair of baggy gray shorts, a red bandanna and the silver chain holding the dog tags she didn't want to remember. But did. Even his feet were naked.

Without warning John spun like a coiled snake striking out for the attack. Instinctively she stepped back, but stilled when she realized that while she saw him, John did not see her. The bandanna. It was tied around his head, over his eyes. Blindfolded like that, oblivious to her presence, the man who she'd desperately wanted to be a stranger continued to execute some sort of martial arts routine. His sleek body moved with exacting precision, arms streaking out in deadly punches, legs raised in high, breathtaking kicks. All the while he balanced on the width of those two old boards. One misstep and he would have no chance to recover.

The quickening started low and spread fast, swirling out to touch every part of her. To make her heart slam and her throat go tight. She told herself she should look away, but couldn't. Told herself she should announce herself, but didn't want to. He might stop then—and she very much did not want him to stop.

She'd heard the term masculine grace, but she'd always thought it an oxymoron. The men in her family were many things, but graceful was not one of them. Now she watched the fluid movement of Detective John D'Ambrosia and realized she'd been wrong. Like poetry in motion, but with none of the frills. Only strength. And restraint. And precision. A mass of energy concealed by the thinnest of veneers.

She didn't have to wonder what else his strength and stamina extended to. She already knew.

The cool breeze swirled around her, but heat seared deep. Too easily she could see him as he'd been that first night. Feel him as he'd reached for her and urged her against him. His strength should have frightened. It hadn't. It had…seduced.

Leave, she told herself, before he realized her mistake. She never should have come here. But a different need held her in place. He executed a series of high kicks and blocks, then a fluid spin. His arms struck out in lightning-quick moves capable of inflicting great bodily damage, had anyone been on the receiving end. Each seemingly effortless movement bled into the next, as well choreographed as ballet—but with the pulsing force of rock and roll.

The way he kicked out his leg drew her attention to his thighs and calves, the dusting of dark hair there. She didn't want to remember the coarse feel of his legs sliding against hers—but did.

Her breath caught, even though D'Ambrosia, the one exerting himself, showed not one sign of labored breathing. Only the kind of intense concentration that stemmed from patience and discipline.

A hard sound broke from his throat as he executed one last high kick, then spun in a full circle. He then stood unnaturally still, feet shoulder-width apart, and bowed at an imaginary opponent.

"Are you just going to stand there and stare?" came his low, knowing voice. "Or did you have something on your mind?"

Chapter 8

John wadded the bandanna into a tight ball. This was when she went away. When she always, always went away. When he pulled the blindfold from his face or opened his eyes, when he slapped on the light and crushed the darkness. When he pushed aside illusion, and focused on reality.

His heart pounded hard—from exertion, he told himself—but he kept his breathing level. That was part of the challenge. See how far he could push, how deeply he could control. Make his muscles burn, but don't let them shake. Make his blood pump, but never let it spill.

Bring his senses to life, but never let them take over.

She stood along the edge of the old, rotting pier, the one he'd fished from as a young boy, the one his daddy had helped his granddaddy build. Her hair was pulled back from her face, in a long braid he would guess, leaving only a few strands feathering against her jawbone. Her cheeks had color. Her eyes were as dark as the brackish water of the dying lake behind her.

And her jacket, sweet Christ, it was her jacket that got to him. Her jacket that let him know she was real and she was there, that she wasn't some figment of his imagination.

The dark green jacket was big and bulky and it hung from her shoulders, swallowing her slender frame and making her look small and lost in ways John knew better than to trust.

Clenching his jaw, he reached for a bottle of water he'd left on one of the posts. "There's coffee in the house," he said, as if the sight of Saura standing with the weeping willow of his youth framed behind her was the most natural thing in the world. "You look like you could use some."

She lifted a hand to slide a wisp of hair behind her ear, just barely skimming the dark circles beneath her eyes. "Thanks, but I'll pass."

He looked beyond her toward the Acadian-style structure hidden by pines and gnarled oaks the majority of the year. "It's fresh-roasted—"

"I'm not here for coffee."

"I didn't think you were," he answered easily, trying to see her as T'Paul had described, as a blond or a redhead. Women who changed their appearance and moved in T'Paul's circles didn't do anything casually. They didn't stop by for coffee. They didn't listen when a cop gave them an order, and they sure as hell didn't ask for permission. Forgiveness maybe. But as John looked at Saura, he almost smiled.

She so did not stand on his property for forgiveness.

"What then?" He glanced at the position of the sun, knew it was time to get back to the house. "Is there a question I can answer? Something you didn't understand last night?"

Like the words: *Stay. Away.*

The change was subtle, hands sliding into the pockets of her jacket, a flicker in her eyes. "The hit," she said, sounding nothing at all like a woman lost or vulnerable, but completely in charge. "It was for you—not me."

Six little words, but they whispered up against him like acid. He felt his hand tighten around the nearly empty plastic bottle, narrowed his eyes toward her. "Come again?"

The cool breeze returned the hair to her face. "The fire… Nathan had it set to take you out. Not me."

"Who is it?" Lambert sounded nothing like the southern gentleman most of New Orleans thought him to be. "The cop?"

Across the phone line, someone answered.

"He alone?" Lambert asked, then, obviously pleased with the answer: "Then do it…take him out."

D'Ambrosia grabbed the small microcassette recorder and crushed the rewind button. "Where did you get this?"

Seated across from him at the butcher-block table, Saura kept her expression as blank as she could. Kept her eyes on the man. The cop. But the fascination wouldn't stop streaming through her. The house, tucked among trees young and old, was…wrong. Austere, as she'd expected. But quaint somehow. Eclectic.

"You have your sources, I have mine," she said, sneaking a glance at the neatly stacked mail on the counter, divided between bills and magazines; the cast iron frying pan drying in a rack beside the sink. The modern coffee-maker. "And just in case you're wanting to think this is a fake," she added, eyeing the two bottles sitting by the stove—one had a whiskey label, the other olive oil. "I can assure you it's not."

The conversation came from her own tapes, produced by the voice-activated equipment she'd stashed in Lambert's neighbor's yard. She'd planted the bugs not in the phone where he would find them, but in obscure places throughout his house. Technology had made tremendous advancements during her time away from fieldwork.

D'Ambrosia studied her for a long moment, then lifted his finger and depressed the play button, allowing Lambert's voice to stream between them again. And again.

The main room off to the left called to her, but Saura kept her eyes on the man. Concentration glowed in his eyes. His shoulders were hard and rigid—and still completely bare. He hadn't bothered to get dressed after leading her inside, hadn't even pulled on a T-shirt. He'd just set his laptop on the counter, flipped a table chair around and straddled it, leaned forward and listened. The perspiration against his chest had dried, leaving only the dog tags hanging from a silver chain.

Frowning, he jabbed his finger against the stop button again and removed the tape, turned it over in his big hands.

"You don't have to believe me," she said, and when she inhaled, the scent of coffee taunted. "That choice is, of course, yours." Slowly, she leaned back and strummed her fingers against the table. "But..." She let a leisurely smile curve her lips. "Let me put it this way. The call comes just after midnight," she said, borrowing his tactic from the night before. "I'm in bed, but not asleep.

"It's Renee," she added, and finally John lifted his eyes to hers. They were dark and piercing, glittering with an awareness as damning as it was daring.

"Cain's fiancée," she clarified, even though Detective John D'Ambrosia would know a detail like that, just as he'd already figured out the grim scenario she was about to paint. "She's worried."

The thought twisted through Saura. "She was with Cain when he got a call," she forced herself to say. Lambert was on to John, wanted him dead. If he chose to ignore the tape... "Something about Lambert and another cop, an ambush—"

"Cute," he said, standing.

But she wasn't about to let him dismiss her. "Not really." And for effect, she, too, stood. But even against her five foot eight, he still towered over her by a good five inches. "Your life is your own, Detective." Smoothly, she reached for the tape and the recorder he'd left sitting next to the oranges. "Live it how you want to," she added as he strolled away. "But know that whatever happens to you won't be on my watch."

At the sleek stainless-steel refrigerator, he stopped and shot her an odd look. "Your *watch?*"

Wrong word. "My conscience." She shifted, questioning the wisdom of coming here. She'd told herself to stay away. To leave him alone. He was a cop. He knew how to take care of himself. And yet Lambert's voice kept playing through her mind. And when she'd finally slipped beneath the covers and closed her eyes, it had been D'Ambrosia waiting for her in the darkness. Then the cold splinters of betrayal. D'Ambrosia moving in slow motion. Reaching for her. Recoiling backwards. Falling. Not moving.

D'Ambrosia's blood—on her hands.

She'd jerked awake, sat up in bed and tried to catch her breath, knew she had no choice. "For not warning you," she said, hating the thickness to her voice. Her throat. "We're even now."

"That's why you're here?" he asked, pulling a half gallon of orange juice from the fridge. "Want some?" He held up the carton. "A life for a life? To pay me back for saving you from the fire?"

Something inside Saura stilled. He made it sound so simple. *A life for a life.* His, for hers. Hers, for his. Once, she'd trusted that illusion, had given it all she had.

"Not even close." Swallowing hard, she watched him pull a beer stein from a glass-front cabinet. "I would have gotten out of the hotel even if you hadn't been there to play hero."

She would have. She. Would. Have. *Somehow.*

She always did.

John put down the glass. He put down the carton of orange juice. Gently, he closed the refrigerator door. Then he turned to her, all six-foot-plus barely-dressed of him, and looked at her, hard, with piercing eyes. And when he spoke, it was with a dead quiet that made her throat go tight.

"That's what makes you dangerous. You really believe that."

The urge to touch him stunned her. To cross the kitchen and lift a hand to his face. His chest. To touch and feel, to see if he could possibly be as hard as he looked.

But then, she already knew the answer.

"You just can't do it, can you?" If her heart slammed hard against her ribs, she chose to ignore it. "Can't say thank you. Can't admit—" The words jammed in her throat.

He didn't move, didn't so much as blink. Just watched her as if she held a still-smoking gun in her hands. "Admit what?"

The sun kept pouring in through the curtainless windows and the birds kept singing. The ping of wind chimes told her the breeze still swirled in from the west.

But something cold and dark moved through her, a truth she wished was a lie. "At Lambert's party—why did you approach me? Why did you come on so strong?"

Now John smiled. It was the slow kind, dark and mesmerizing, like a sunrise but in reverse. "You really have to ask? A beautiful woman—"

"Don't." She pushed away from the table and crossed the hardwood floor to where he stood. "Don't play me for a fool and don't pretend the reason you approached me had anything to do with my appearance." The blade of hurt surprised her. "You came on to me for one reason and one reason only." And it had nothing to do with her. Or them. Or what had passed between them one careless night she wanted to scrape from her memory. "Because I was Nathan's date."

His smile deepened, making his cheekbones look sharp enough to slice. "That was an added benefit."

"And the only one you cared about," she said against the tightness of her throat. "You wanted to use me, didn't you?" It was all so clear now. "You wanted to use me to go after Lambert."

She felt raw and exposed, but D'Ambrosia merely lifted an eyebrow, and reached for the orange juice. "It seemed like a good idea at the time."

She watched him pour the liquid into the stein, waited until he brought it to his mouth before pulling her punch. "You still can."

He stilled, lowered his hand from his face. "Still can what?"

"Use me." Her heart slammed hard with the words, the dark images that immediately formed. She stepped closer, but didn't touch. That would be too easy. Too predictable. Too much like the night before, when D'Ambrosia had backed her against the door and taken her hand. Instead, her overly sugary smile was slow and deliberate, and she took a moment to appreciate Detective D'Ambrosia with his back against the wall.

Or in this case, the counter.

"You can't go near Nathan anymore," she pointed out, acutely aware of the heat radiating from his big body—and soaking into hers. "He has your number. He wants you dead. But me—"

"No."

"He has no idea who I really am. What I want. He doesn't know I was at the hotel—"

"Yet."

"It's called a window of opportunity. I can—"

A hard sound broke from his throat. "You can what?" He moved so fast she had no time to prepare. No time to brace. "Get close to him?" he asked, taking her hand and bringing it to his body, splaying her palm against the warm flesh of his chest. "Touch him like this?" With the question his expression shifted, and he raised a hand to her body. And put his palm against the side of her neck. "Let *him* touch *you?*"

Her breath caught. And her throat burned. D'Ambrosia was a man of precision and control. Of discipline—and denial. But there was nothing precise or controlled about the glitter in his eyes. Nothing disciplined about the possessive edge to his voice.

No denial about the way he touched her.

On a deep coffee-drenched breath, she looked up and felt the rush clear down to her toes. "It's a chance I'm willing to take." A chance she had to take.

His fingers stiffened against her throat. "I'm going to pretend you didn't just say that."

The words, or maybe it was the way he said them, low and quiet without so much as one sliver of emotion, fired through her. "You can pretend all you want to," she said equally low and quiet. "But it doesn't change the truth, Detective. You need me."

His body tensed.

"So badly it scares you," she added even more softly, and with the words, stepped closer.

For a moment he said nothing. Only looked at her. Looked through her. As if he could reduce her to a puddle and make her go away with nothing more than a hot stare.

Then he moved his hand, sliding his palm along her shoulder and down her arm, and despite the thick fabric of the jacket separating flesh from flesh, she would have sworn she felt every callous. "I'm not the one scared here, *belle amie,*" he said. "I'm not the one who ran away."

Now his hand slipped beyond the jacket to her wrist, where his fingers curled, and his thumb began to rub. From defense to attack in less than one broken heartbeat.

"What are you afraid of?" she pressed, not about to let him turn the tables on her. "And don't give me some bull story like you did last night." When he'd made it explicitly clear just how big a risk she'd taken—and how shattering a mistake she'd made. "I know what I'm doing. I—"

His hand closed around hers. "You have no idea what Nathan Lambert is capable of."

"And you do. Yes," she said, not even trying to keep the frustration from her voice. "So you keep telling me. But you might be surprised at what I know."

"What you do or don't know doesn't change the fact that I don't need a partner."

Partner. The word caught her by surprise. She'd insisted that D'Ambrosia needed her, wanted him to use her. But never once had she thought of what they could achieve together as a partnership. Didn't want to think of it that way now.

"Because of Alec," she whispered, startled by the quick play of emotion across D'Ambrosia's face, the anger and the regret and the—guilt. "He was your partner." And now he was dead.

He released her hand and moved away from her, crossed the kitchen and braced his hands against the edge of the sink.

She knew better than to follow. She knew better than to reach out—

"Don't." He twisted toward her, and with absolutely no warning or transition, the anguished man vanished, replaced by the stone-faced cop. "Don't pretend like you have a damn clue what I'm thinking, and don't pretend we're in this together. We're not. I'm a cop. You're not. And I meant what I said last night. Stay away from Lambert."

"You'll be watching. Yes, I know," she said through yet another wave of frustration. "But there won't be anything you can do, will there? Because you can't get close to him, and I can." And that was the bottom line. She could accomplish what he could not. "Which means you can't stop me without putting us both in danger."

He leaned against the counter, crossing his legs at the ankles. "Is that another risk you're willing to take?"

The urge to give him a good hard shove surprised her. "What? You think just because you can shoot a target blindfolded and do your little martial arts dance on your pier without falling into the lake means you don't need help? That you're invincible?"

"Prepared," he said. "There's a difference."

"Prepared for what?" She tried not to notice the play of sunshine and shadows against his face. But did. "Operating in the dark?"

"For anything." The cleft in his chin deepened. "For everything. For Lambert—for you."

At least that's what he wanted to believe. But he hadn't been prepared for his partner's death. For being there when he died, but not being able to change the outcome.

"Operating in the dark," he was saying, "keeps your senses alive."

It was an odd statement coming from the man who'd looked at her from across the voodoo-queen's-cabin-turned-dive with absolutely no life whatsoever in his eyes.

"And you think that makes you a good cop," she guessed. It was the only reason a man who wanted to feel nothing would work so damn hard to keep his senses sharp.

"Sharply-hewn senses make me good at a lot of things," he said, grabbing a neatly folded dish towel from the counter. "You of all people should know that."

She did. In cruel, explicit detail. That was part of the problem.

He took the towel in both hands and held it out to her. "Would you like to try?" he asked, stepping toward her. "See what it feels like to rely on nothing but touch and sound and scent?"

Her body responded, sending a rush of heat swirling through her. Without her eyes, she would have to rely on her hands to guide her. She would reach out, and he would be there. She would touch, and she would feel. And even as she spun away she would still hear the sound of his breathing, still teeter dangerously close to drowning on the scent of soap and sweat and leather and man.

She took the towel—and dropped it to the floor. "This isn't about me." It was about Alec—and bringing down Lambert.

John's eyes took on a slow burn. "I'm afraid that's where you're wrong," he said. His gaze dropped along her body, and despite the jacket concealing her curves, every nerve ending quickened. "I may be a cop, but I'm also a man," he said as he lifted his eyes back to hers. "And when the instincts of one collide with the needs of the other, it's smarter to indulge, than to ignore."

Indulge. The word whispered through her like a seductive promise—or an even more seductive threat. "Be very specific here, Detective. Just what are you indulging by trying to keep me away from Lambert? Instinct—or need?" She let a beat of silence spill between them before continuing. "The cop?" she asked. "Or the man?"

For a moment he did nothing. Said nothing. Just stood, more naked than not, and watched her with a gleaming intensity that made her heart thrum low and hard.

Then, slowly, a smile curved his mouth. "Who says there's a difference?"

He did, whether he knew it or not.

"Would you like me to go into more detail?" He stepped toward her. "About my needs—my instincts?" Lifting a hand to her face, he skimmed his fingers along her cheekbone. "The questions that play through my mind when the lights go off?"

Once, when Saura was seven, her uncle Edouard took her hunting. She'd fought him every step of the way, had no desire to see anyone raise a gun to a deer or rabbit, and pull the trigger. But Edouard had insisted. Saura could still remember the moment they'd seen the doe in the clearing, drinking from a stream. She'd looked pretty and peaceful, and maybe Saura had read too many stories, but all she could think was that the deer was someone's mother. That she had a baby somewhere. Waiting for her to come back to her. As Saura herself had once done.

But mothers didn't come back from suicide.

She'd frozen, watching Edouard lift the rifle and bring it to his face, squint through the sights and slide his finger along the trigger.

Then she screamed.

Standing in the middle of D'Ambrosia's oddly quaint kitchen, she thought of the deer, knew how it must have felt in that one moment when she'd glanced up and caught sight of man and gun. The moment before she'd bolted into the woods.

D'Ambrosia didn't have a gun trained on her, at least not one with bullets. But his quietly spoken, deliberately explicit questions had the power to destroy—and he damn well knew it.

"Nice tactic," she said with a calm that belied the fight-or-flight rhythm of her heart. She knew what he was doing, using sex to blur the issue and scare her off. For effect, she lifted her hands, and clapped. "Very smooth."

"Should I take that as a no?"

"Take it any way you want." Turning, she strolled to the table and picked up her purse, told herself it didn't matter that he would think he'd succeeded in scaring her away. Maybe that was actually better. Let him think he was in control. She'd accomplished what she'd set out to. She'd given him the tape.

And in doing so, she'd received much, much more.

With a wistful glance at the main room she'd not gotten a chance to explore—the huge leather recliner and old chintz-covered sofa, the small television and neat stack of magazines on a pine table, one of her brother's photographs on the wall near a shadow box—she turned back to D'Ambrosia. "I gave you the choice, Detective. Remember that."

Then she headed for the door through which he'd let her almost an hour before. She pulled it open and welcomed the cool swirl of the breeze, swallowed hard when his hand came down on her wrist. "This isn't a game."

Bracing herself, she turned to him one last time. "I'm well aware of that."

"Are you?" His voice was different. "Are you sure?" Still low and dark, but pulsing, not flat. Smooth, not rough. "Is that what you tell yourself when you let Lambert touch you?" he asked silkily. "When you used to parade around the French Quarter as a blonde or a redhead?"

Chapter 9

The question slammed into Saura. He knew. Somehow, some way, he'd learned her secret. Knew of her past.

"Is that why so many people think you're dead?" he went on in that same quiet voice. "Because you know when to play and when to back off?"

Ripping her hand from his grip, she did back away. A stranger, she remembered thinking. *Her* stranger. A man just passing through. Who didn't know who she'd been or what she'd done. Who could not touch her. Could not hurt her.

Did not have a weapon lifted to her heart.

She could not have been more wrong.

"I wish that it was," she whispered against the burning of her throat. "Do what you have to," she added as the breeze from the pecan trees slapped a few strands of hair into her face. "But respect me enough to let me do the same."

The muscle in his cheek started to pound, and when he reached for her again, she stepped back. Again.

"This isn't about respect," he said.

"No, it's not." The words were soft. Calm. But inside, the chaotic threat twisted through her. The game she didn't want to play had just shifted.

Knowing what had to be done—*the only thing that could be done*—she walked away.

He didn't try to stop her.

He looked like death warmed over. That was John's first thought when Gabriel Fontenot pulled open his door. The assistant district attorney with the fabled poker face had a reputation for cracking witnesses as easily as he could turn a worthless hand of cards into a profit. That was the Robichaud in him. Armed with evidence or flat-out bluffing, no one ever knew. The finesse came from his mother's side. Or so rumor had it.

Robichauds didn't waste time on finesse. Not when they wanted something.

And Saura Robichaud definitely wanted something.

Frowning, John shoved aside the thought and focused on the man squinting at him through bloodshot eyes. The man who usually wore designer suits but now wore only a threadbare New Orleans Saints division championship T-shirt—*that* hadn't happened in a long time—and a pair of faded jeans. His feet were bare. Rolled-up newspapers littered his porch. His face needed a razor. His hair needed scissors. And from the looks of him, he could damn well use a cup of coffee. Or ten.

"Didn't mean to wake you," John said.

Gabe lifted his hand to his face and rubbed. "You didn't."

John glanced beyond him, into the small uptown house Gabe had shared with his fiancée. The lights were off and the blinds shut, but through the shadows he saw the bar separating the kitchen from the main room, the carton of Chinese on the counter. And the handgun. It was small and silver, several years old he would guess. Next to it lay bullets. Three, he counted.

And something inside him went horribly, brutally tight. "Gabe—"

"I got your messages," his friend said, pulling the door open wider. "You want to come in?"

Playing it cool, feeling as if he was walking a thin, dark line, John stepped into the cool darkness of Gabe's house. Once, the decor had been a swank combination of antique and post-modern. Now on a quick glance John saw the walls stripped of all art. Several pieces of furniture gone. No candles or framed photos or other knickknacks that screamed of a woman's touch.

And in that one awkward moment, John thought of Saura, of her quirky little row house, and wondered if she knew just how broken her cousin was.

"How's your mom?" he asked, because he wasn't quite sure what else to say. "That new security system working for her?"

Relief flashed in Gabe's eyes. "So far."

"Any luck convincing her to move?" Her house had been broken into three times in four weeks. But nothing had ever turned up missing. "She really needs to get out of there."

"I told her that," Gabe said. "Uncle Eddy told her that. Cain told her that. But once her mind is made up, it's made up. She's not about to be run out by some bored teenagers with too much time on their hands."

"I've got a couple of black-and-whites passing by pretty regularly," John said. "That should help."

"Thanks." Gabe veered into a kitchen so austere that John's looked downright homey. No magnets on the refrigerator. No salt and pepper shakers or fruit or—anything but dishes in the sink. And an empty bottle of whiskey. Next to a small, amber prescription bottle. "Care for a drink? I probably have a beer—"

"On the clock," John said, cringing at the cold recognition that slid into Gabe's eyes. It had been almost ten weeks since he'd been on any kind of clock, since he'd put on a suit and slipped behind the wheel of his BMW, driven to the courthouse.

Looking away, Gabe pulled open the fridge. "Water, cola—"

"Gabe." John didn't think twice about stakeouts or kicking in doors. He could lay it on the line for informants and comfort victims. He could interrogate and he could grill, he could make defense attorneys wish they'd never called him to the stand. But standing there in that depressing kitchen, he didn't have a damn clue what to do for his friend. Pretend he didn't see what he saw. Confront it head-on. Thump him on the back.

Knock some sense into him.

Saura would hug him. She would march right up and pull him into her arms, hold on as tight as she could. Then she would give him hell.

"I'm not here for a drink." Or small talk, despite the fact that he'd been the one to initiate it.

Gabe pulled a bottle of water from the fridge and closed the door. "Have you found her then?"

John glanced at the pistol, back at Gabe. "Not yet," he

said, hating the frustration that tightened through him. "But I have a few leads."

"Maybe there is no woman," Gabe said. "I didn't see—"

"I saw her." Could still see her, a tall woman with white hair, moments after the explosion, running from the warehouse Alec had walked into. "She's real, and she was there."

And he'd bet his last dollar she'd seen something. That she knew something.

Gabe let out a rough breath. "If that bastard had anything to do with Alec—"

"I'll prove it," John finished for him. That was what he could do for Gabe. Find the evidence to bring Lambert down. "Gabe—" he said again, more awkwardly this time. But he couldn't not say anything. Couldn't just leave it alone. Couldn't stand at another man's funeral and for the rest of his life wonder…

"What the hell is going on here?" he asked, crossing to the bar, where the pistol lay with its chamber spilled open.

For a moment Gabe said nothing, just walked to stand beside John and stabbed a hand into his uncombed hair. "It was hers," he finally said, without one sliver of emotion. "I found it while looking for laundry detergent."

John closed his eyes, opened them a moment later. Gabe was a good guy. He hadn't deserved what happened with Val—and he sure as hell didn't deserve for reminders to keep cropping up. "You want me to take it? Bring it down to the station?"

Gabe nodded. "That would be great."

The little blast of relief was juvenile and he knew it, but John briskly went about getting a plastic bag from the cabinet, then securing Val's pistol. That he knew how to do.

"I met your cousin," he said, sealing the bag. "Saura."

Gabe lowered the bottle of water. "Saury? Is she okay?"

It was an odd response to a simple statement. But then, John *was* a cop, and Gabe *was* an attorney. They were trained to look for the dark side. "Fine," he said, "at least for the moment."

"I worry about her," Gabe said, then took another swallow of water. "She's been through hell."

John tensed, felt something cold slide through him. He knew the basics. Saura had been engaged, and her fiancé had been killed. She'd gone into seclusion after that, prompting those who'd known her face but not her name to think she, too, had died.

But damn it, the need to know more twisted through him. She'd been hurt. Badly. By the look he sometimes caught in her eyes, he'd say devastated was a better word. But she was back now, nonchalantly flirting with danger in the name of bringing Alec's killer to justice, driven by something that John didn't understand—or maybe he did.

It's her death wish I'm worried about.

"That's what I hear," John said, seizing the opening. Sometimes you really could kill two birds with one stone. "And I'm hoping you can help make sure it never happens again."

Marcel Lambert's lakefront home was every bit as beautiful as his brother's. The charming two-story, built in the style of a plantation home, dominated a heavily treed lot that sloped down to Lake Pontchartrain. The home had been in his wife's family for decades, but after Katrina they'd done extensive renovations, sparing no expense as they selected the finest marble and granite and wood, fixtures that cost more than many New Orleaneans made in a week.

At the far side of the back room, a wall of plate-glass

windows showcased the view of the lake. "It's really something when a storm comes in," Caro, Marcel's wife was
saying, while Saura studied the stone path trickling down
to a boathouse. Despite the strategically-placed solar lights,
little else could be seen. The trees were too dense. The
shadows too thick.

"I'll bet sunrises are spectacular," she said, returning her
attention to her hostess. There was no one standing in the
shadows. No one watching or waiting. That was only her
imagination. And yet deep inside, she shivered.

Two days had passed since she'd seen D'Ambrosia—
but his words, his threat, lingered.

If you…breathe the same air that man does, I'll know.

"Amazing," Caro answered. "Sometimes Marcel and I
take our morning coffee on the verandah and—"

"I'm sure our guest is not interested in our morning
coffee," Marcel said, smiling indulgently as he took his
wife's hand and pressed a kiss to her knuckles. A famed
restaurateur who frequently appeared on morning news
shows, Nathan's younger brother knew how to use a smile
as effectively as he did cayenne pepper.

"But if I can steal you away for a few minutes, the
reporter from the *Picayune* just arrived. She'd like to ask
you about the ice sculpture."

Caro's eyes brightened. "Yes, of course," she said,
flashing Saura an apologetic smile as her husband led her
away, leaving Saura alone with Nathan for the first time
since she'd arrived. He'd sent his chauffeur to pick her
up, had called at the last minute explaining he had a few
unexpected calls to make and would need to meet Saura
at the party.

Now he took her hand in his and drew it to his mouth.

"Have I told you how happy I am you decided to join me?" he asked. "I've been worried about you."

Her smile was authentic. She was happy to be there, as well. Happy to be near Nathan. Happy to have a chance to learn whatever she could—even if she couldn't shake the feeling she was being watched. "You're too good to me."

Looking elegant as always in his glowing white tuxedo shirt with black bow tie, he squeezed her hand. "No," he said in his richly cultured voice. "You are the one who is too good to me."

She wasn't sure what made her heart kick. Wasn't sure why she abruptly looked across the room. Why everything inside her tensed.

Until she saw him. He emerged from a group of well-known lawyers and judges and started toward her with none of his usual composure. His eyes were—wrong. They were dark and shuttered, wild somehow. And his hair. It was parted at the side like always, falling against a cowlick at his forehead, but it was too long. And his face—he needed to shave.

Not D'Ambrosia. But her cousin. Gabe.

Uneasiness quickened through her as he approached with recognition and disbelief hot in his eyes. "If you'll excuse me—" she started, but it was already too late.

Gabe blocked her retreat. "Lambert," he stunned her by saying. From the tight set of his unshaven jaw, she'd expected him to literally yank her away from Nathan—one of two men Gabe's sister swore she saw in their father's study the night he allegedly committed suicide.

"What's the matter?" Gabe taunted, raking his gaze over the shimmery silver dress that hugged all the way down her body. "You have to slip down yet another generation to find a woman who can't see straight through you?"

Nathan's eyes went stone cold. "Fontenot," he said. "Finally decided to show your face again?"

"Just remember," Gabe said, and Saura's heart moved into an uneven rhythm. Not one trace of recognition. Not one sliver of familiarity. "When this one gets done with you," he slurred, smelling so strongly of whiskey it was as if he'd splashed it against his throat instead of cologne, "you so much as touch anyone under eighteen and you'll find yourself behind bars faster than your money can—"

"Easy there," Nathan interrupted smoothly, pulling a small phone from his pocket. "Let me call your uncle. He can send someone for you—"

"Leave my uncle out of this." Gabe shot Saura a quick, hot glance. "If I so much as hear a rumor that you've come anywhere near my family—"

His words broke off so abruptly Saura knew something had killed them. She followed the direction of his hard gaze, and saw the woman. Tall, slender, swingy brown hair. Intelligent eyes. Locked onto Gabe's.

Evangeline Rousseau was her name. She was an A.D.A., just as he was, with the exception of integrity. Gabe had it. Not only had she set him up for a hard fall, she'd come horribly close to getting him killed in the process.

The urge to protect wound deep. Saura wanted to charge across the room and tell the other woman to stay the hell away from Gabe. Make it explicitly clear what would happen if she did not. The Robichauds had influence around these parts—

But Saura could not move. Could not say a word. Because she was not a Robichaud when she was with Nathan. She was Dawn. A simple woman with stars in her eyes.

"Ah, yes, your family," Nathan said with buttery insincerity, and Gabe swung back toward him, eyes no longer bleary, but hot and hard and one hundred percent lethal.

"How *is* your mother?" Nathan asked. "I heard she'd had some trouble lately. Some break-ins? And your sister. I was so relieved to hear that waitress killed down in Florida didn't turn out to be our dear sweet Camille."

Everything inside of Saura stopped brutally. She wanted to slip a hand onto Gabe's forearm and stand with him, take Nathan's thinly veiled threat and spit it back at him. Even more she wanted to pull Gabe aside and ask him what the hell was going on. What he was doing at the party. Why he was offering himself up to Lambert for target practice. And most importantly of all, why he pretended he did not know her.

Except as soon as they formed, the thoughts fell together, and the answer whispered through her.

"Good try," Gabe said with a hint of the attorney he'd once been, his smile so razor-sharp Saura's breath caught. "But you won't win." He looked at Saura, let his gaze sear into hers. "The name is Gabriel Fontenot," he said, sliding a hand into the pocket of his sport coat—not a tuxedo— then pulling it out and pressing a business card into hers. "And if this man so much as looks at you the wrong way, you have only to call me, and I'll be there so fast you won't even have a chance to breathe."

In that moment, she wasn't sure she'd ever loved her cousin more. Or hurt for him more. There was a jagged ache in his words, a pain in his eyes she wanted to chase away.

But with one last look at Lambert, he strode away, straight toward Evangeline Rousseau. Saura watched her eyes go wide, saw her take a step back as Gabe closed in on her, took her wrist and practically dragged her out the sliding glass door into the darkness of the patio.

"Well," she said with a breathlessness that wasn't the least bit forced.

"You'll have to excuse him." Nathan's smile was apologetic. "He's a lost cause. I'll go find security, have him removed from the property."

"No, it's all right." Smiling uneasily, she scanned the guests in their tuxedos and cocktail dresses, wondering how she could feel a man she could not see.

You can't get close to him, and I can...

He was there. Somewhere. Somehow. In the shadows. Watching. He'd sent her cousin to keep a public eye on her, but Saura knew D'Ambrosia would not have been content to hand over the reins of his investigation to another man.

"Excuse me, Mr. Lambert?" A waiter with dark brown hair and killer cheekbones slipped beside two restaurant critics and eased next to Nathan. Balanced on his hand was a tray of cocktails. Tucked inside his tuxedo jacket, Saura saw the telltale bulge, and knew this man was no waiter at all. "Your brother asked if you could join him for a few minutes."

The change was subtle, an alertness moving into Nathan's gaze. He glanced across the room, then at Saura. "I'm sorry—"

"Go," she said with a warm smile. "I'll be waiting."

With one last lingering glance he walked away, but the waiter remained a heartbeat longer than he should have. He looked at her, almost looked through her.

And that's when it clicked. She'd seen him before, at Nathan's party. He'd been posing as a waiter then, as well. As soon as the moment broke and he left, she slid her hand into her evening bag and pulled out a small receiver, subtly lifted her hand to her ear and inserted the device.

Courtesy of a matchbook she'd slipped into Nathan's pocket, the voices came to her immediately. She moved as well, crossed to the foyer and slipped into a burnt-red powder bath. Closing the door, she turned on the water and listened.

Guests mingled everywhere. In the foyer. In the parlor and dining room. Even at the base of the main staircase. Everywhere she went, people were there. They saw her. They would remember. And if asked, they would tell Nathan exactly where she'd gone.

Saura kept her pace ambivalent, her smile warm. When a waiter passed, she snagged a glass of chardonnay. But she did not drink, wasn't about to let anything soften so much as one edge. All the while her heart raced, fueled by a dark rush that had been silent for too long.

"It's Dawn, right?"

The soft voice came from the right, and she turned to see a young woman with long dark hair and big soft eyes approaching her. She'd seen her earlier, had noticed her immediately. Despite her copper silk gown and the diamonds dripping from her ears and around her neck, she looked oddly out of place. Like someone who wanted to belong, who was trying to belong—but didn't.

"Have we met?" she asked.

The younger woman flushed. Much younger, Saura realized upon closer look. She doubted the girl had seen her twenty-first birthday. "No," she said with a hesitant smile. "I'm Darci."

Saura forced a smile, so categorically did she not have time for chitchat. "Nice to meet you," she said glancing

beyond the girl, toward a staircase tucked near the kitchen.
"Will you be around later? I was just on my way—"

"No, no that's okay. You're here with Mr. Lambert,
right? I was wondering if you'd seen his brother."

Something inside Saura quickened. She heard the hesitation in the girl's voice, saw the discomfort in her eyes.
"Not in the past few minutes," she said. "You might check
with his wife—"

"No, that's okay." Darci turned and hurried away, reminding Saura of the doe that autumn morning, the one
that had bolted into the woods the second Saura called out
her warning.

The urge to go after the young woman was strong, but
not as strong as the urge to slip upstairs. Later, she told
herself, with a quick glance to make sure no one was
paying attention to her. Later she would find the girl. Later
she would give her a smile and make her comfortable, find
out what she didn't want anyone to know.

Now Saura slipped down the hallway bisecting the
second story, noting closed doors on both sides. Four to the
right. Five to the left. There would be bedrooms. Probably
a bathroom. Maybe a closet. Open the wrong door—

She sensed him before she heard him, the way everything inside her stilled and gathered. With a hard kick to
her heart she spun, found him closing in like a fast-moving
storm. A very dark, very dangerous storm. He was on her
before she could step back, taking her not by the wrist but
by the hand, and leading her not into the closest room, but
to the third door on the right. Leading her. Not dragging.

And the door, he closed it softly, when every tight line of
his body screamed that he wanted nothing more than to slam.

But Detective John D'Ambrosia did not slam. Ever.

That would signify a loss of control, of concentration. It would mean something had gotten to him. And that, Saura knew, was not something this man could abide. He didn't want to care. He didn't want to feel. He just wanted to—

Not to hurt.

The realization brought an ache *she* didn't want to feel. She watched D'Ambrosia standing with his back to her and his hand curled in a death grip around the glass doorknob, watched his shoulders rise and fall beneath the long-sleeved black T-shirt—didn't understand why he wouldn't look at her.

Didn't understand why she wanted him to, so very, very badly.

"John—" she said. Not *D'Ambrosia*. And wondered if he noticed. Then she beamed a smile. "We've *got* to quit meeting like this. People might start to—"

He turned to her slowly, revealing the hard set of his jaw and the dark light in his eyes. His hair was shorter than it had been that morning, cut with the same razor precision that ruled every aspect of his life. The control—God, the raw control he was exerting. She could feel its tight edges from four feet away.

"Do you know what room you were standing outside of?" he asked with a roughness that touched her in ways and places she didn't want to be touched. "What door you were about to open?"

She chose to ignore that he obviously thought she was incompetent enough to open without checking first for voices. "The one with Lambert inside?" she guessed.

"And his brother," he said, locking the door. "And two bodyguards." Now he moved toward her, the tidy room of lavender walls and small white furniture making him look bigger somehow. "Do you need me to go on?"

Maybe she should have backed away, but doing so would have brought her to the frilly canopy bed.

"He knows," she said, going on offense instead. Logic told her to keep her distance, but she closed in on him and destroyed the distance between them. And touched him. Lifted her hands to his arms and dug her fingers into soft cotton and hard muscle. "He knows you're here."

She would never know what made D'Ambrosia's eyes glitter—the way she touched him, or the revelation she dropped at his feet. "What are you talking about?"

She pulled the small disc from her ear and handed it to him, recounted what she'd heard. *This must stop,* Marcel had said. *The risk is too high!* He'd almost sounded…scared.

John took the receiver and stared at it, then at her. "This is how you knew about the fire? You've bugged him?"

In another time, another situation, the incredulity in his voice might have made her laugh. All her life she'd been dismissed, seen first as a nuisance, then a trophy. Men had assumed that just because she had a fondness for fashion she must not have a brain in her head. That she didn't see things, notice things. Hear things. That she didn't know how to leverage an advantage—and overcome a weakness.

She'd taken great satisfaction in proving them wrong.

But as she looked at the punishing combination of concern and admiration in D'Ambrosia's eyes, she could find no laughter—and no pride.

"He wants you gone," she said over the hard thrumming of her heart. "This time for good."

Swearing softly, he lifted the disc to his ear. "That's not going to happen."

"This place is crawling with security. We've got to get out of here before they find you…" And eliminated him.

The silence screamed in from all directions, hard and jagged and brutal, throwing her back to the night she opened her door to find her brother standing grim-faced on her porch. She'd known before he'd spoken a word, had felt the bottom drop from her world. He'd reached for her—

Swallowing hard she destroyed the memory and focused on John, standing so still, staring at the little girl's bed as he listened to the Lambert brothers' conversation. She didn't know how he could do that, stand so still not even his breath moved through him. The green of his eyes almost looked black. "John—"

Something wild flashed in his eyes. Without warning he took her hand and tugged her across the room.

From down the hall a door opened. Then closed. Footsteps sounded on the hardwood floor. Brisk. Determined. Moving closer. And voices, low and muted and—

Everything went dark. And quiet. She strained against it, but could see nothing. Hear nothing. For all of one frozen heartbeat.

Just as quickly the moment lurched forward, and John was gathering her against his body and dragging her through the darkness. Across the room to a door, which he pulled open as the footsteps intensified, no longer walking. But running.

And from somewhere downstairs, the sound of a woman's scream. And shouting. Then her name, not the one on her birth certificate, but the one she'd given Lambert. *"Dawn?"*

And she knew. She knew who was opening and closing doors in the hallway. Why he was running. What he wanted.

What would happen if he found a locked door, if he kicked it in to find her crouched in a closet with the man he wanted dead.

She had no choice. None at all. Not if she wanted to live—not if she wanted John to live.

On pure blind instinct Saura jerked from the warmth of John's arms and ran across the room, lunged for the door.

Chapter 10

John ran. Hard and fast, from the closet and across the soft beige carpet. It wasn't that far, no more than ten feet, but with each stride something inside him shouted. Quietly. Fiercely. Because he could not shout with his voice. He could not call to her, tell her to turn around and come back to him.

To stay the hell away from Nathan Lambert.

Because Nathan Lambert was just outside. Looking for her. If she suddenly appeared, rushing from the room and into his arms, full of some story about being lost—

Nathan would pretend to believe her. Maybe even pretend to soothe her. But he wasn't stupid. And he couldn't afford to take chances. No matter how badly he wanted Saura, he couldn't take her story at face value, not after security had reported someone casing the house. That's why they'd killed the power…

"Dawn!"

John caught her at the door, his body caging hers, his hands reaching for her arms. She stiffened but did not fight, didn't protest as he lifted her and carried her back to the closet.

"Sweetheart, it's okay," Lambert was saying. "I know you're probably scared but—"

Silently, John closed the door.

"—you have to trust me."

He could hear her breathing. Feel her heart slamming against his shoulder. Feel her, all of her, warm and sinuous, draped over his body.

The urge to slide her to her feet and back her against the row of clothes, to lift a hand to her face and—cradle—stunned. The urge to put his mouth to hers and obliterate all the recklessness, all the ill-conceived courage, to make her forget about Lambert and Alec and whatever dark passions drove her, stunned him even more.

"…you can put me down…" she was saying. And something inside him snapped.

"Are you out of your mind?" It took inhuman restraint to keep his voice quiet, because there was nothing quiet inside him. He released her and slid her to her feet, not letting her touch so much as an inch of his body. "What in God's name did you think you were—"

"Unlocking the door."

The quiet, emotionless words stopped him.

"If he'd found it locked he would have known—"

The door to the room opened. "Dawn? Sweetheart?"

A beam of light streaked in from the space between the door and the carpet.

John backed her against the hanging clothes, pulling her behind them, next to what felt like a hanging net. And through the stillness she relaxed into him, put her head to his chest and slipped her arms around his waist.

The closet door opened. "Dawn?" The light swept down the center. Then the darkness returned, and the door closed.

But still, neither of them breathed. Until the outer door opened, and closed. And the footsteps, as well as the deceptively cultured voice, moved away.

"John," she whispered against his chest. *"John."*

It took a moment for her voice to register.

"…can't breathe."

It was only then that he realized how tightly he held her, that he had his hand stabbed into her hair and her head pressed against him, holding her—

He released her and felt her stagger back, heard her drag in a rough breath.

He should have left her alone. He knew that. He should have let her back away from him, put distance between them. He should have stood there still and quiet, and waited.

Reaching for her was foolish. And weak. But he could no more not reach for her, not touch her again, than he could stop breathing. He lifted his hands through the soft fabrics hanging from the closet and found her only a few feet away. Then his hands found her shoulders and he slipped them around to her upper back and stepped toward her, tried not to crush.

The kiss was hot and hard and needy, fueled by denial and restraint and the lingering threat of death. She tasted of wine. And courage. And a fear that touched him somewhere deep inside, a fear that made him want to protect—

"No," she said, and then she was struggling, turning her face from his and pushing against his arms. "We can't do this."

"Saura—"

"You have to let me go," she said, fumbling for his hands. She found them and dragged them from her body, squeezed. Then again, quieter. Grimmer. *"You have to let me go."*

Everything inside of him went hard and tight. "Go where?"

"Back to him."

The words were quiet, matter-of-fact, and John wasn't sure he'd ever wanted to put a fist through the wall more.

"He'll keep looking for me," she said with a cold logic that he hated, and now her hands released his, slid along his arm to his shoulder. "If he comes back—if he finds us together—"

All bets were off. John knew that, hated that she was right. No matter how badly he wanted to, he couldn't keep her there with him, had to let her go. If he didn't, if Lambert came back and found Saura in John's arms…

He could pull his gun. He could fast talk. He could claim he'd dragged her in there against her will. Claim she was too stupid for her own good, that she and Lambert deserved each other. Shove her into the other man's arms.

But in the end, none of that would matter if Lambert's henchmen surrounded them. In working against her, in trying to stop her, he'd only succeeded in compromising her.

Through the darkness he could see nothing. But he *could* feel. Her body pressed to his, the rise and fall of her breath and the thrumming of her heart, her fingers at his jaw, and something else. Something inside. Something hard and sharp, that just kept splintering—

"John." She slid her thumb to his bottom lip. *"Please.* You know I'm right."

A hard sound broke from low in his throat. "Do you have any idea?" He ground the words out. "Any idea at all what it does to me to see the two of you together?" He'd stood just beyond the windows, looking in at the two of them cozied up across the room. And sweet Christ, it had taken every ounce of training, every molecule of control, to stay where he was. "The way he looks at you," he added, "touches you?"

Against his throat, he felt her breath. "Do you have any idea what it does to *me?*"

The resignation in her voice ripped at him in a way he hadn't expected. Didn't want. "Then stop."

She pushed back, leaving a sweep of little girl's clothing to fall against his face. "I can't!" she said. "Not when I'm this close. Don't you get it, John?" Despite the fact she kept her voice low, determination tightened around every word. "I can do this. I'm what you need— all you have to do is use me—"

"Don't." This time it was he who moved, he who shoved from the wall and found her standing in the middle of the closet. "Don't ask me to use you."

She stepped into him and again reached for his hand. And again, squeezed. "Then *help* me," she said. "*Help* me bring Lambert down. *Help* me make Alec's killer pay."

His chest tightened. She made it sound so damn easy.

"We can," she said, softer this time. "Together we can make Lambert fall, make sure he *pays*. He doesn't suspect me."

This time it was a growl that broke from his throat. And this time, it was need that won. He pulled her back into his arms and brought his hand to her face, put his mouth to hers, and drowned. For a long, long time. He waited for her to push him away. But she didn't. She slid her arms around his neck and opened to him, kissed him back. Not with anger or frustration as she'd kissed him earlier. Not with the urgency or desperation from after the fire. But with a gentle acceptance, a quiet sadness that shredded everything he thought he knew about her.

Knew about himself.

"Then go," he said against her seeking mouth. Then he slid his hands to her shoulders and pushed her away. *"Go."*

She did. Without a word. Without turning back. She opened the closet door and vanished into the darkness, ran for Lambert. Leaving John alone in a closet of frilly little girl clothes and stuffed animals, trying like hell to breathe.

"I don't want to say good-night."

"You're sweet."

"Trust me. There's nothing sweet about the way I'm feeling."

Silence. Thick and dark and punishing. Then a sound, low and raspy and leisurely. Mouth against mouth. Body to body.

Years of training allowed John to remain where he was, refusing to allow a muscle to so much as twitch. But he could do nothing about the violence pounding through him. Whether by design or accident, Saura had not retrieved the receiver she'd pressed into his hand, enabling him to listen to her every word, every breath, for the rest of the evening.

Listen to the soft lies with which Lambert plied her.

And worse, the soft silence, when John's imagination filled in the blanks. Now they stood just outside the door of her fake apartment, and Lambert very clearly wanted in.

"Nathan," she whispered with a wistfulness that made John want to put his fist through the door. "I'm sorry, but I think maybe I had too much champagne. My head…" She let the words trickle off, followed them with a little laugh. "I'm afraid if I don't lie down soon…"

"Then you shouldn't be alone."

John tensed.

"I'm fine," she said. "Really." Then another blast of silence. "Give me tonight," she whispered. "And I'll give you tomorrow."

John's hands curled into tight fists. In that dark place inside, the tightness was even worse.

"Tomorrow, then," Nathan said, and when the silence came, John knew that he was kissing her.

The sound of a key sliding into a lock had never been so welcome. The door came open and the alarm he'd bypassed blared. Saura slipped inside and closed the door, slid two chains into place before deactivating the alarm. Through the shadows he saw her close her eyes and lean her forehead against the wall, realized just how much her charade cost her.

"I'm here," he said, and she twisted toward him. But didn't move. Not toward him, not away when he closed the distance. She just watched him through the most bruised eyes he'd ever seen, went quietly into his arms. And held him. Tight. As if she never wanted to let go.

Breathing her in, John buried his face in her hair and closed his eyes, wondered how the hell he'd find the strength to do what had to be done.

She didn't want him to leave. The realization whispered through Saura, even as she inventoried all the reasons she needed him to. She didn't want to see him there in her house, on her sofa. And she really was tired. Everything had started spinning shortly after she'd left John and found Nathan downstairs, let him pull her into his arms and promise her everything would be okay. The electricity had come back on—he'd claimed a fuse had blown—and the party had swirled on.

But Saura had been unable to shake the sensation that something had shifted—nor could she forget the scream. Someone was overreacting, Nathan said, but Saura had to wonder.

Just as she had to wonder when the spinning had really started. There in the darkness of Marcel Lambert's house, or days and weeks before, in the darkness of another room…?

Refusing to go there, she carried two cups of hot chocolate into the small living room of the house she'd rented on the outskirts of the Quarter. Built over a hundred years before, all the rooms lined up in a straight row, with a long, narrow hallway running down one side to connect them.

"I'm afraid I don't have any beer or soda," she said, stepping onto a braided rug. The words were horrifically trite considering all that remained unsaid between her and John. She had no idea how long they'd held each other, only knew that her throat had gone tight the second she'd seen him, that her heart had slammed and bled, begged. Wept. Because in that one frozen moment, she realized she'd never needed anything more than she'd needed his arms around her.

For so long there'd been only Adrian. During the years since his death, she'd jerked herself awake and pulled her knees to her body, sat in the darkness, hugging herself, but imagining him, feeling—nothing.

It was the nothing that had destroyed. The nothing that had driven her out of her house six weeks before.

The nothing that had driven her into a stranger's arms.

Adrenaline, she tried to tell herself now. Relief. That's why she'd wanted him to hold her tonight, because of the letdown that invariably came at the end of a roller-coaster ride, when your feet hit solid ground and you knew you were safe. That's when you sagged. That's when you shook. She'd just been so tired of acting and pretending, staying on guard. And then she'd finally gotten rid of Nathan, found John waiting.

Do you have any idea what it does to me to see the two of you together?

She'd expected anger. She'd expected a lecture or reprimand. Instead he'd come to her through the darkness and opened his arms, held her against the warmth of his body and given her tenderness. The combination had destroyed.

It was also yet another reason why she needed him to go.

Standing near the antique secretary, he turned to her. "I'm not that thirsty—" he started, but his expression closed when he saw the mugs in her hands.

She stopped. "Is something wrong?"

The short cut of his hair—a Caesar cut, she'd heard it called—accentuated the severity of his eyes. "No, I just—" Maybe it was supposed to be a smile, but the tightening of his mouth looked like a grimace. "It's been a long time since I've had hot chocolate."

She tried to give him a smile in return, but his words scraped through her, exposing a truth she didn't want to see.

It had been a long time since Detective John D'Ambrosia had done a lot of things. Touch. And feel. Relax.

And drink hot chocolate.

"It's good for the soul," she told him, as her grandmother had told her. But the second the words left her mouth, the second the cleft in his chin deepened, she realized her mistake.

When she'd first seen him, all those weeks before,

sitting alone across the room, her first thought had been of isolation. He'd reminded her of one of the cypress trees her brother loved to photograph—still and stoic amidst an ecosystem that had turned its back on him, that was slowly choking out his brethren, until only one remained.

She'd thought the comparison silly, until she'd seen his eyes. Soulless, she remembered thinking. Damaged.

And now she'd just offered him a cup of hot cocoa, thoughtlessly claiming something as benign as chocolate and marshmallows would be good for his soul.

What he needed, what his soul needed, was far, far more than a candied drink.

"John—" she started, but before she could step toward him the moment passed, vanished actually, and he indicated a small, framed photograph.

"Cain and Gabe?" he asked.

The picture sat prominently on the old secretary. She'd placed it there on purpose. She passed it every day. But she almost never looked at the faded image from nearly a quarter of a century before. It sat there as a reminder, an albatross.

Now she made herself look at the picture, and saw what she usually tried to avoid. The past. The laughter and the innocence and the hope. Untainted, untarnished, unblemished.

"A long time ago," she said, setting the two mugs on the coffee table. Throat tight, she crossed to John and took the frame in her hands, felt the echoes whisper through her.

"Who's the girl?" John asked. "A friend?"

Now her hands wanted to shake, and now the echoes screamed. She forced herself to look anyway, to see. The girl. Five years younger than Saura with surprisingly blond hair and blue eyes. Just like her daddy, but not at all like the other Robichauds. Saura remembered the day she was born; it had been like getting her own living, breathing baby doll. "Camille," she whispered, and the name hurt. She hadn't spoken it aloud—

She didn't know when she'd last spoken it aloud.

"Gabe's little sister," she said.

John crowded in behind her, looking over her shoulder. "I didn't know Gabe *had* a little sister. Is she—"

"No," Saura answered before he could say the word. She didn't want to hear it, refused to consider that her cousin might be gone, and none of them had been there to say goodbye. "She…doesn't live here."

"Pretty," John commented. "Where does she live?"

It was a simple question, casual, as close to small talk as she and John had come. But standing there looking down at her cousin's faded smile, Saura closed her eyes against the hot surge of moisture, and wanted. So much. Her cousin to be okay. To come home. To know that her family loved her, didn't think that she was crazy. To know that someone believed her, that her father's memory had been restored. His murderer punished.

John put a hand to her arm. "Saura?"

She inhaled slowly, but the wanting didn't go away. It deepened and spread, beyond the past and her cousin, to the present and the stranger. Who wasn't a stranger. Who'd touched her when she'd been quite sure she could never be touched.

"No one knows," she said, turning to look at him.

The reality of him standing so close, of his face being within inches of hers, made her heart pound. It would be easy to step into him, feel him against her.

"It's been a long time," she said, and for a moment wasn't sure to what she referred. Since she'd felt, or since her cousin had vanished. "Thirteen years…she was just seventeen."

John took Saura's hands and squeezed. "Tell me."

She looked up at him, at the green, green of his eyes, and felt something inside just…release. Felt it let go. He was a cop. A detective. He lived to solve puzzles. Forming theories was what he did. But he did none of that now, jumped to no conclusions, simply held her hands and asked her to tell him.

"She saw her father murdered," Saura surprised herself by saying, and with the words, vertigo took over. She felt herself sway, felt John steady her, felt him take her hand and lead her to the sofa.

"When she was thirteen," she said, easing down and folding her feet beneath her. But the room kept spinning.

Because of the past, she told herself, the image of Camille as she'd been found the morning after, wet and cold, in the hollow of a tree at the back of the Robichaud property. Jacques had burst out of the woods, holding her and shouting—

"But no one believed her," Saura said, not wanting to return to that time, not wanting to feel or dwell. She'd run with them, had called the ambulance. Had stayed with Camille. Held her. "They said she was confused, mistaken. Scared. That Troy Fontenot took his own life. That no one else had been anywhere near."

Against John's face, the shadows deepened. "Gabe's dad committed suicide?"

"No." The word practically shot out of her. "Uncle Troy would never—" She broke off and stared at the picture, of Gabe and Camille and Cain, taken only a few days before the bullet shattered everything. "What kind of man would do that to his children? What kind of man would choose to leave them, to abandon them, to let them grow up alone, without a father to—"

John's eyes went dark. He looked away from the picture, away from her, toward the window across the room. Against his knees, his hands curled into fists.

Saura felt the loss clear down to her soul. Without stopping to think, she put a hand to the denim covering his thigh. "John?"

For a long moment he did nothing, just kept looking into the night. The tightness of his jaw emphasized the shadow starting to set there, despite the fact he'd been clean-shaven earlier in the evening.

But it was his eyes that got her, his eyes that made her yearn. They were grim and…damaged.

"John?" She turned into him, but didn't lift her hand to his face as she wanted to, realized that no matter how badly she wanted to touch, now was not the time to do so. "Did I say something?" she started to ask. But stopped when she realized that she had. Said something.

What kind of man, she'd asked, *would do that to his children? What kind of man would choose to leave them, to abandon them, to let them grow up alone, without a father to—*

The answer wound around her heart, and squeezed. John's father, she knew. John's father had done that.

He closed his eyes and opened them a heartbeat later, not to the man who'd led her to the sofa, and not to the boy who'd been abandoned by his father, but to the hard-edged detective who drove himself, who lived his life to make sure those who hurt others, paid the price of their sins.

And Saura couldn't help but wonder who he was punishing. Himself? Or the father whose absence had shaped John into a man whose damaged eyes belied the tenderness that seeped into his hands.

"She vanished thirteen years ago? Four years after her father died?" Standing, he paced away and stopped at the photo. "And no one has heard from her since?"

Saura followed him. "For a while she sent cards, to me and Gabe and her mother, for our birthdays. And for Christmas."

"Then there would be postmarks—"

"They never led anywhere."

"Someone would have seen her—"

"Don't you think I know that?" she asked, feeling the twist of it all over again. The hope—and the disappointment. The leads that led nowhere. The fruitless phone calls and e-mail messages. "That's why I went to Little Rock and Naples and Muncie, to Normal." After every card. Until they'd stopped. "To every post office. Every train and bus station…"

It took a moment to realize John had stopped staring at the picture, and now stared at her. *"You?"* he asked in a quiet, fascinated voice she recognized too well. The kind of voice her uncle and brother used when someone had just slipped up and given them a piece of information they very much wanted, but didn't yet understand. *"You* looked for her?"

The urge to step back streaked through her, but she knew he would only come after her. "She's my cousin. I love her."

"Your uncle is sheriff," John pointed out. She could almost see the pieces shifting against each other, trying to form a picture in his mind. "Your brother was a cop. Your family has money. You could have hired an army of private investigators—"

"They did," she said. "At first. My uncles had the cops all

over it." Saura had been out of her mind with worry—and guilt. "Pretty young girl gets in her car to drive to New Orleans, but never arrives. Her car is found three days later down by the river, stripped. No sign of the girl, nothing missing from her room, no clothes or makeup or jewelry—"

John frowned. "They suspected foul play."

"She was young, vulnerable, a Robichaud—a picture-perfect target. Uncle Eti was convinced there would be a ransom note. Edouard and Cain weren't so sure, thought maybe Camille herself had been the target, not the family bank account."

"And you?" John asked. "What did you think?"

Saura thought of the carefree smile on Camille's face. "After Uncle Troy died, after the authorities insisted she was wrong, that no one had been in the study with him, that he put the gun in his mouth of his own volition, Cami was never the same. It was as if something inside her…died."

It wasn't until over a decade later that Saura had learned how lost and broken her cousin had felt. How alone.

"At school, some kids started to call her Crazy Cami, but she never fought back, never seemed to care." That had been Cain and Gabe's realm. And Jacques's.

But as far as Saura knew, no one else knew about the nightmares. She'd woken Camille from them, held her and rocked her, promised her everything would be okay. "When she left—when she vanished, I couldn't help but think, what if she'd been right? What if that bastard really did murder my uncle? What if he was afraid Cami would remember his face? His voice? That someday someone would believe her—" Slowly, she looked up and met John's gaze. "What if he'd come back for her, covered his tracks once and for all?"

Dim light played across the lines of John's face. "You thought your cousin's disappearance had to do with her father's death." It was a statement, not a question, and with it came a wave of acceptance she hadn't expected.

"But no one would listen to me. Except Gabe. He felt like hell for dismissing her when she tried to tell him, for insisting she was just confused, that she'd imagined everything."

John swore softly.

"He went after her," Saura added. "And so did I." There'd been no leads, but she'd refused to let that stop her. For years she'd been slipping in and out of shadows, extracting information no one wanted her to have. It was as if every breath she'd been taking had been preparing her to help her cousin.

Somewhere in the distance, a train horn sounded. "What happened?" John asked.

She lifted a hand to shove the hair from her face. "The first cards came, to Gabe and Aunt Gloria and me. Camille telling us that she was sorry. But that this was how it had to be. She was safe. She left on her own accord. And she wasn't coming back." Fleetingly, Saura glanced at the bottom drawer of the old secretary, where the card sat in a box with every other piece of correspondence she'd received from her cousin. "*That* is when the investigation changed. The police lost interest, and my uncles called off the investigators, retained only one or two to keep their eyes open for a runaway."

"They just let her go?" The disbelief in his voice almost soothed the edges of the memory.

Saura swallowed. "I told them they were making a mistake, that we couldn't just give up on her, that we had to—" She could still see her uncles standing so tall and powerful and utterly unyielding. She'd wanted to shove them. To scream at them.

Instead, she'd taken matters into her own hands.

"We let her down," she said quietly. "*I* let her down. I was her cousin by blood, but her sister in every way that mattered. I promised her I would take care of her, be there for her, but—"

He didn't let her finish. He caught her arms and looked down at her with an intensity that made her pulse surge a little too fast. "You did *not* let her down."

"But I did," she said. "I knew Cami never recovered from losing her dad. I knew she'd been ostracized, that people pointed and laughed at her, that she would wake up screaming…" Saura squeezed her eyes shut, opened them with a harsh breath. "I promised her. I promised her I would be there for her—"

"And you have been." The words were strong, his voice tender. "For thirteen years you've looked for her."

And she couldn't take it. Couldn't let him slay her with a tenderness she neither anticipated nor wanted. A concern that made her feel small and fragile in ways she'd vowed to never be again.

"That's just it," she said, twisting from his arms. "I couldn't even get that part right. I searched for her until—" She looked away, felt the burn clear down to her bones.

And again John touched her, his fingers to the underside of her jaw, urging her face toward his. "Until what?"

Until life got complicated. Until she fell in love and got careless. Until Adrian died, and everything fell apart. "It doesn't matter," she said against the tightness in her chest. This wasn't what she wanted from John, damn it. Compassion and concern. Tenderness. The combination swirled through her like a seductive drug and made her want, made her remember. What it felt like to be alive—what it felt like to love. To lose.

"All that matters," she said very quietly, "is that the bastard who destroyed my cousin's life is still out there. Still hasn't paid, still walks free—"

John went very still. And against her face, his fingers tensed. *"Saura."*

Just her name, that was all he said. But he might as well have stripped off her jeans and sweatshirt, her bra and panties, left her standing there painstakingly naked. Because his voice told her that he saw. That he knew.

"Tell me," he said very slowly, and his eyes practically glowed. "Tell me who killed your uncle."

Chapter 11

Saura had two choices. She could pretend, or she could take a leap of faith. Standing in the muted lamplight, she looked up at John, the shadows across his face and the strength in his eyes, the conviction in every solid line of his body, and for the first time in a long time, she didn't want to pretend.

"Lambert," she said, lifting her chin. "Nathan Lambert killed my uncle."

For a moment John said nothing. Did nothing. Remained as he was, one hand curved around her shoulder and the other against her jaw, and looked at her. Looked hard. Looked and reminded her what it was like to not be alone.

Then he turned away and took a few steps, stopped abruptly and shoved a hand through his hair. "Christ, Saura—"

"Don't." This time it was she who moved, she who went to him and curled her fingers around his forearm. "Don't tell me I'm wrong," she said. "Don't tell me I don't know what I'm doing, that I'm playing with fire. And don't you dare tell me to back off."

"If Lambert finds out you're a Robichaud—"

"He'll kill me. Yes, I know." She stepped closer. "But he won't find out."

The cleft in his chin darkened. "You don't know that. Your family is well known, you're in the spotlight—"

"*They* are. But *I'm* not. *You* didn't even know. *You*—a cop who's friends with both my brother and my cousin."

"Goddamn it," he snapped. "That's different. I didn't have any reason to suspect—"

"No," she said, trying not to drown in his scent, in memory. In truth. "You had no reason to suspect. You saw only what you wanted to see, what was easy to see." Just like everyone else. "A lonely woman. One whose name you didn't know, didn't want to know. Someone you could hold onto then let go of without looking back."

"I'm not the one who walked away."

"But you would have," she said with amazing calm. "Because that's what you do, isn't it? Walk away. Stay uninvolved."

Validating her point, he gave no reaction to her words. "This isn't about me."

Once Saura had been a woman who felt everything with an intensity that had often gotten her in trouble. She'd been called reckless and restless. Life had been for exploring, and she'd explored. It was as if she'd always been in search of something, that until she found it she would never be satisfied.

Until Adrian. With Adrian she'd felt whole, and satisfied.

And then he'd died, and for two years, Saura had felt nothing at all. Until John. She'd approached him in the bar not out of the brash passion which had once driven her, but a numb desperation. To see if she could feel again. If she could want. If the woman she'd once been still lived, or if the bullet that killed Adrian had killed her, too.

The answer stunned her. From the beginning John had awakened her body. But with his simple question—the disappointment, confusion and yearning bleeding through her—she realized the awakening extended beyond the needs of her body.

"No, it's not," she agreed, and somehow her voice didn't break. For a foolish, dangerous moment, she'd slipped. And she'd wanted. Him to understand—him to be different. Him to feel the same irrational need that she did.

"It's about me," she said. "The truth. What people see—and what they don't."

What he had seen. And more sobering, what he *hadn't* seen.

He almost seemed to wince. "Talking in riddles—"

"Forget it." She'd already said too much—and he hadn't heard any of it. Hating the way she felt inside—raw and exposed—she walked to the window, stared out at the clay pots on her front porch. The butter-yellow pansies looked scraggly. They needed water.

"Saura."

Again he spoke only her name. But the way he said it—rough and...tentative, maybe even frustrated—carried an intimacy that rivaled the way he touched her with his hands.

Slowly, she looked from the plants to his reflection on

the glass. The urge to retreat from the intensity in his eyes was strong, that knee-jerk reaction from looking dead-on into the sun. But the curiosity was stronger.

"Tell me," he said, and the words swirled through her like a dangerous drug. "Tell me what people see…what they don't."

He was a cop. He knew how to interrogate. He knew how to vary his technique based upon his subject. He would know when to keep his distance and circle close. It was all a matter of getting what he wanted.

She knew all that. But none of it overrode the longing. It unfurled through her like a frayed ribbon and though she could think of a hundred reasons to open the front door and stand there until he left, she shifted her gaze to the night beyond, and did exactly as he asked.

Because she couldn't remember the last time anyone *had* asked.

"When I was little," she said, and although her heart pounded, her voice was quiet, "I could smile and kiss my uncle on the cheek, curl up on the sofa with a book, and within minutes he would forget I was there. He would make phone calls or review cases, leave his notes on the coffee table—notes he hid when my brother walked in." Until Cain got older. "But that he never hid from me. Never thought I would even look at."

That fact had hurt…until she'd learned to use it.

"Do you have any idea how easy it was?" Through the window she watched him. "There's a man in a bar or a restaurant, maybe at the track. He's guarded, maybe even packing. Looking over his shoulder. But then there I am, asking for directions, or maybe asking for the time, always with a smile."

The man in the reflection tensed.

"It's like taking candy from a baby," she added as an old Cadillac wheeled around the corner one block down and cruised toward them, lights bright and hip-hop music blaring.

Now he moved, so fast she wondered if he ever did anything slowly. In one smooth motion he lunged for her and practically dragged her from the window, had her body pressed against the wall and his gun in his hand long before the beat-up car moved into range.

The Caddy cruised right on by. But still John didn't move, barely breathed. He knew he should relax, quit crowding Saura against the wall. No shots had been fired. It had only been his own goddamn paranoia, the fea—

No. Not fear. Fear had no place in this. It was the certainty, the head-on instinct of the cop that made it impossible for him to stand down around her.

That he kept his arms around her had nothing to do with how damn bad he'd wanted to touch her, with the ache he'd seen in her eyes, the pain she concealed behind a sensuous smile.

"How long?" he gritted out, wondering how the hell she could have been invisible to anyone. Ever. Because she wasn't invisible to him. He could see her in vibrant, punishing detail, and what he saw almost made him forget everything he'd taught himself about survival. Everything his father had taught him.

"I was seventeen the first time," she said. Her candor made him wonder how long she'd been waiting for someone to listen.

"My uncle had been investigating a forgery ring," she was saying. "He'd nailed a few underlings, but no one would talk." Her smile was low, smug. "Until I found a courier in a pool hall, and let him buy me a beer."

John squeezed his eyes shut, opened them a long moment later. "Your uncle…did he know?"

A low gleam moved into her eyes. "He knew he got information and made his bust, sent a finder's fee to a post office box."

Back away, John told himself. *Back the hell away.*

"And you had the satisfaction of knowing you'd done something he couldn't do."

Dark hair fell against her face. "I had the satisfaction of knowing I could make a difference. That I could take what everyone thought of as a weakness and use it to my advantage. It was the most incredible rush I'd ever known. But it wasn't until Cami disappeared—"

Her words stopped, and silence poured in.

Shifting, John eased away to brace his arms against the wall on either side of her. He was a trained interrogator. He knew how to extract information. But as he looked into her haunted eyes, he realized it was the man in him who wanted her to keep talking. The man who'd first seen her across the smoky barroom. Who'd let her touch him, when he'd been sure that he could never be touched.

That he never wanted to be touched.

The cop, the one who could wear down the most unrelenting of suspects, who knew how to survive, told him to end this right here, right now.

"What happened when Cami disappeared?" he asked.

She looked at him a long moment before answering, as if searching for a cue card with all the right answers. Then her expression softened. "Something inside me changed."

With the words she slipped from beneath his arm and moved away from him. And he let her go.

At the secretary she stopped and ran her finger along the glass door. "My puzzle solving went from a game to a calling," she said. "It took over and defined me. It was like every time I hit a brick wall with Cami, I had to score a touchdown for someone else. To prove that I could. That I was—"

Worthy. She didn't say the word, but it was there in her face, there in the way she seemed so lost and alone in her own home, the way she'd tried to hide the tears after they made love. And it stabbed through John with a precision that disturbed him on too many levels to count.

She skimmed a lock of hair from her face. "The first time Cain used me—"

"Your brother knows?" he asked before she could finish. Somehow, it didn't fit. And somehow, damn it, he didn't ever want to hear her talking about being *used* again.

"No." Her eyes sparkled, knocking fifteen years from her face and distancing her even further from the sultry vamp from six weeks before. "I always worked through a series of covers," she said. "No one in my family ever had any idea who *Femme de la Nuit* was."

Everything inside of John stilled. *"Femme de la Nuit?"* he whispered in a strangled voice he hardly recognized. Denial came next. With her hair tangled around her face, Saura's bulky sweatshirt and faded jeans made her look so damn close to the girl next door it made his chest tighten. That she was speaking of the once notorious private investigator as if she were saying absolutely nothing of consequence was too incongruous.

"Sweet Mary." All the misshapen pieces slid into a

picture so crystalline clear and brutally sharp that the truth of it sliced through him. No wonder T'Paul thought she was dead. They all did.

"You were *Femme de la Nuit.*" Lady of the Night. Bold. Fearless. One hundred percent thorough.

"I still am." Her fleeting half smile damn near ripped out his heart. "Just a little rusty."

He knew the stories. He knew her track record. He'd heard the speculation—the lady of the night had been a hot topic of debate among the boys at the station. They'd taken bets—just how did she get her hands on information no one else could? How far would she go, how many lines did she cross? Were her charms reserved for men only? For one at a time? Or would she do whatever it took?

Christ, John bet on the latter: no limits, no lines, one partner or two, male or female or both. Whatever it took.

Now, blood roaring, he slipped a hand into his pocket and pulled out the listening device she'd given him, the one which had allowed him to torture himself with sounds of her and Lambert. And finally it all made freaking sense. "You're playing a dangerous game."

A game she'd played many, many times before.

The girl next door vanished, replaced by the smooth, confident lady of the night. "*We* are," she corrected, somehow looking taller. Sleeker. More in control. She crossed to the window and eased back the curtains. "He yours?"

Christ, even her voice was different. Lower. Stronger.

And John didn't need to stand beside her to know what she saw. Who she saw. He'd seen T'Paul earlier, slouched down with a bottle in a paper bag on the porch of a vacant house across the street. "Yes."

Her smile surprised him. It was slow and daring and so

damn provocative it was all he could do to remain where he was. She seared him with it, let the moment stretch into a long, taut line between them.

Then she moved to the door. "It's late," she said with a fake yawn. "What time should I expect you tomorrow?"

In other words, he was dismissed. Taking his time John crossed to her, and now he permitted himself to touch. He lifted a hand to her face and eased a tangle of hair behind her ear, let his fingers linger against the curve of her cheek. "What makes you think I'm going anywhere?"

She lifted her eyes to his. "We both know you can't stay."

The truth of her words should have slapped him into reality. He couldn't stay. He knew that. Didn't want to stay. That's why he'd let her go that first night—and why he'd been trying to get rid of her every night since then. Because when he was with her, all he wanted to do was touch. And taste. And keep. Everything else faded—the promises he'd made and the vows he ruled by, the blood-stained memories that drove him, punished him, even after the passing of over twenty years.

But holy God, one look at the pain and courage in her eyes, and all that just—disappeared. "Why not?"

Her eyes changed, shifted from the glimmer that haunted to a dull glaze that punished. "Because that's not what you do."

The simple statement stripped him bare. She looked at him as though she could see everything. *Everything.* As though she knew, and she pitied.

"That sounds like a dare," the cop in him said, taking over. The cop knew what to do, knew how to draw lines— knew how to clean up the mess the man had made six weeks before.

Her chin came up a notch. "Are you saying I'm wrong?"

His thumb slid from her cheekbone to her lower lip. "Do you want to be?"

She did as he'd expected—as he *wanted*—and reached for the glass knob and pulled open the door. But then she smiled—*smiled,* damn it, as if rather than calling her bluff, he'd amused her somehow. "Nathan is picking me up at 7:30."

The urge to back her against the wall and—

He didn't know what. He only knew that she was wrong. He was wrong. For the first time in he didn't know how long, he didn't want to leave. He didn't want to go. He wanted to step *toward* her, not away; he wanted to taste, to carry her to the bed, and this time, damn it, this time he didn't want her to cry.

This time, he wanted to know that she made love to him, not a stranger.

The thought fired through him, sent him striding into the cool night air. But then he stopped. And then he turned.

"There's something you should know." At the dead quiet of his voice her eyes flared. "You were wrong," he said. "Earlier—when you told Lambert good-night."

He wasn't sure what he wanted, but Saura said nothing, just kept the door half closed between them, and looked at him as if he'd suddenly pulled a knife on her.

Walk the hell away, the cop instructed. But the man stayed and made another misplaced vow. "He can't have tomorrow."

Saura blinked. "What?"

"Tonight," he said. The confusion in her voice drove him. "When Nathan brought you home. You promised if he gave you tonight, you'd give him tomorrow."

He moved without warning, giving her no time to slam the door on him. With two steps he conquered the distance between them and took her face in his hands. And then his mouth was on hers and he kissed her with the hard possessiveness of an addict falling off the wagon. On a low growl he tore away and looked down into her eyes, all wide and damp, realized how damn easy it would be to drown. So he refused to let himself see. And he refused to let himself want.

But most of all, he refused to let himself need. "That's not going to happen."

On cue the cop returned, and he walked away.

Saura didn't watch him go. She closed the door and secured the locks, shut the blinds and switched off the lamp, walked into the kitchen.

For so long there'd been nothing. No interest or motivation. No anticipation or curiosity. No passion. No disappointment.

No pain.

For someone with the excitable blood of her Cajun ancestors, the abrupt cessation of every emotion had been like living without a life force. She'd awakened every morning and gotten dressed, walked through her day as everyone else did. She said the right things. Did the right things. She ate and drank and breathed, but inside, there'd been nothing.

Shock, one of the kinder doctors had said. Grief, her family believed. And maybe they'd all been right. In losing Adrian she'd lost more than the man she'd loved. She'd lost hopes and dreams. She'd lost her future. And a child.

Closing her eyes, she put her hands to the flatness of her stomach and felt the stab of pain all over again. No one had known, not Adrian, not her. When her period failed to come during those long cold weeks after she'd buried him, she hadn't thought twice about it. Grief was like that. But three weeks turned into four, four into five, and then the nausea came. And the dizziness.

She'd been nine weeks along when the doctor confirmed her pregnancy. And for the first time since Adrian's death, she'd wanted to live again. She'd cared. She'd started to eat regular meals and drink lots of water, take long walks through the woods.

And then the baby had died. Just like that. With no warning, no cramping, no spotting. Wearing a new pair of stylish maternity jeans, she'd gone in for her first sonogram and lain there awaiting the moment she'd heard so much about, when a woman saw her baby for the first time. There would be pictures. She could carry it with her at all times, pull out the black-and-white image and see that something of Adrian still lived.

But the technician grew very quiet, and turned the screen away from Saura.

And in that moment she, too, had died. Again.

And she'd stayed that way for a long, long time. Until Renee Fox came to town and proved that lives could go on, that happiness could bloom from the ashes of sorrow. Saura had watched her brother come back to life, had watched the love grow between him and Renee, and she'd started to wonder, and want. Nothing specific, simply a vague sense of longing. She'd *wanted* to *want,* and that, she'd figured, had to count for something: a start, maybe, like the first few drops of water melting from an icicle.

The only shoes she knew to step into were those she'd once worn, so she'd picked up the threads of her old life and vowed to find the truth about Alec's death, and to once again look for Camille. Somehow, both had felt…right.

D'Ambrosia wasn't part of the plan. She didn't want to want *someone* again. She only wanted to be *Femme de la Nuit.* She wanted to do what she knew how to do, what she was good at. What wouldn't crater her all over again.

She wanted to *want,* not to *feel.*

But now, God help her, every time she so much as thought about D'Ambrosia, everything inside her exploded like a kaleidoscope of color. She wanted—and she felt.

And it terrified.

Saura opened the refrigerator and pulled out a bottle of water. She'd been afraid before. When her father died, then her mother. When she'd wandered into the swamp looking for a fabled treasure and got lost. When at fourteen one of her uncle's friends had wandered drunkenly into her bedroom and started slurring about how much he could teach her—

To this day she didn't know who had frightened her more—her uncle, or her brother. Clutching the sheet to her chest, she'd realized for the first time they were both capable of murder.

Her fear had changed after that, matured. She'd begun to see it as a challenge, a test, and she'd come to crave the taste of conquering it.

Until one well-placed bullet taught her that sometimes what you fear most pales in comparison to reality. It was that reality she didn't want to live through again. She didn't care if anyone thought her a coward.

Taking a long sip of water, she crossed the kitchen to the mail sitting on the counter. Absently she thumbed through the newspaper flyers, the bills and a decorating magazine addressed to the previous owner. Then she saw the envelope. It was small and white, her name and address neatly typed across the front. None of that made her heart pound. But the upper right corner did.

There was no stamp, no postage mark.

Going very still, she reached for a tea-stained dishtowel and used it to hold the envelope as she slid a knife along the seal. From inside she withdrew a single sheet of note-paper. On it were nine neatly typed words.

STAY AWAY FROM LAMBERT—OR YOU COULD BE NEXT.

John could be brutal. And John could be harsh. He could be crass, but he could also be elegant. And kind. Whatever the situation warranted, the cop could produce. It's how he kept his solve rate so high—and how he stayed alive.

Unlike his father.

Mike D'Ambrosia hadn't known how to be anyone other than who he was, and he hadn't known how to separate his life as a cop from his life as a man. A father. He'd just been Mike, idealistic and bighearted, an altar boy turned beat cop who believed if he went to church every Sunday and provided for his family, if he followed the rules, everything would be okay.

And it had been, until the day he'd answered a domestic violence call and made the mistake of turning away from the seemingly distraught father to check on the small child who lay whimpering on the sofa.

One mistake. One misjudgment. So many lives changed.

Sitting in a tattered wingback chair covered in a faded floral fabric, John forced himself to give the old woman a soft, sympathetic smile. But inside frustration wound tight.

She was so lying.

"You're sure you didn't see anything?" he asked.

Violet Hebert shifted uncomfortably. They sat in the front room of her small house on the outskirts of the Garden District, she on an old camel-back sofa in the same rose-covered fabric as his chair. Behind her, sun spilled in through the gauzy sheers and glinted off the white of her hair.

It was hard to believe this docile grandmother in her homemade dress was the woman he'd been seeking since the explosion. Three separate witnesses placed her at the warehouse in the days prior to the fire. One placed her there the day of.

"I am surely sorry, Detective," she said, her lyrical voice that of the Old South. "I do wish I could help you. But I was frightened after the explosion." She glanced at the metal detector propped in the corner of the room. According to her story, she'd been at the warehouse as part of a regular sweep of the old industrial area.

"I—I know I should have come forward and let the police know I'd been there, but I was…frightened."

John was not in the habit of interrogating little old ladies, especially with pictures of her entire family, past and present, looking on from the top of a grand piano in need of a paint job. Uncomfortably cramped in the small chair, he let his knees fall open and leaned forward.

"Frightened of what? If you didn't see anything…" He let the words dangle, the question clear. If she didn't see anything, didn't know anything, why was she afraid?

She clasped her hands. "I am an old woman," she said in that way his grandmother had often used, feigning weakness with a strength that had once made his back go straight. "But I am not a fool." Nervously, she glanced away before continuing. "Warehouses don't just explode, Detective, and bad guys do not take kindly to witnesses."

"Violet," he started, but when disapproval filled her eyes he corrected himself. "Mrs. Hebert. You don't have to be afraid." Still leaning forward, he opened his hands in a pleading gesture. "We can help you. We can protect you—"

"Like you protected that man?" The question was sharp, and with it she stood, moving away from the window and wrapping her arms around her frail body. "With all due respect, Detective, I saw the news stories. I know what happened. A man died—"

John stood. "Not just a man, Mrs. Hebert. His name was Alec, and he was my friend."

She turned toward him, lifted wary eyes to meet his. "Your friend? Is that why you're here? As a friend, not a cop?"

The question scored a direct hit. "His wife is a good woman." He sidestepped the query. "She deserves to know the truth."

From somewhere beyond the small room came a soft thud, and Violet's eyes widened. John spun and took an instinctive step, but before he even hit the foyer a wiry gray tabby bolted into the room and scrambled to the top of the sofa.

"Francois!" Violet admonished with a soft clucking noise. "I declare you are going to be the death of me yet."

John watched her cross to the cat and run her hand along its fur, but he'd been a cop too long for the sight to automatically soothe him. He'd been on too many stakeouts, walked through too many allegedly deserted buildings. He'd heard too many muffled thuds, had dreamed his father's death too many times.

"I truly am sorry," Violet said again. Her smile was the

epitome of genteel politeness. "But there is nothing more I can tell you."

Nothing more she *would* tell him, John corrected silently. Because she was right. If Lambert found out she'd been in the vicinity of the warehouse the day it blew, in all likelihood her house would go up in flames within hours. And despite the protection John had promised her, he knew that until Lambert was brought down, Violet Hebert would never be safe again.

Nor would Saura.

The thought ground through him. They'd talked earlier, confirmed plans for tonight. In just a few hours she would again resume her place on Lambert's arm. Listening to every word, John would be close enough to make sure the scum didn't try to get her anywhere closer than his arm.

"I understand," he told Violet, because he did. He crossed to her and pressed his card into her surprisingly strong hands. "My cell number is on the back. If you think of something, anything, you can call me anytime."

The little black dress hugged in all the right places. Saura looked at herself in the bathroom mirror, trying to reconcile the woman who stared back at her with the woman she'd been for the past two years. The woman who'd worn jeans, T-shirts and flip-flops, not designer dresses, sheer nylons and stilettos.

The loud knock at the bedroom door killed her musings. "You said five minutes," John reminded.

She had. Ten minutes ago. "Almost ready," she told him, but still did not move. In truth she was ready, at least technically so. For Nathan. But for John…

It had been a long time since she'd dressed while a man

waited in the other room. It was silly and she knew it. John's presence should have made no difference. They had a working partnership. But as she'd slipped from her sweats and stood in the bathroom wearing only a pair of panties and a bra, her thoughts had been of him, standing so rigidly near the sofa. Of the Glock she'd seen holstered around his shoulders.

She'd offered him a soda—he didn't want one.

She'd flipped on the TV—he'd flipped it off.

She'd handed him a magazine—he'd tossed it on the sofa.

Concentration, she'd realized. He'd already been readying himself for the night and didn't want to break his thoughts.

She'd tried to find the same concentration, but as she'd removed her underwear and reached for the black lacy set she'd picked up that afternoon, her thoughts had returned to the man in the other room. What would it feel like for him to—

She'd broken the thought, but others had formed, when she'd slipped into her dress and run her fingers through her hair, when she'd put on her lipstick.

For Alec, she told herself, with one last glance in the mirror. She'd dressed for Alec. Not for Nathan, and not for John. The two of them were simply means to a very important end.

From her bed she picked up her handbag and crossed to the door, thought briefly of the cryptic note instructing her to stay away from Lambert. Threat or warning, she didn't know, but either way, she'd not mentioned it to John. There was always the chance he'd sent it himself, to scare her away or test to see if she'd tell him about it. She didn't want to think that but could not dismiss the possibility. Nor could she dismiss the certainty that if John did not send the note and she did tell him about it, he would call tonight off. And that she couldn't let happen.

If, however, he did send the note and she didn't mention it to him, then it was yet another of his tests that she'd failed. And that, she figured, was probably for the best.

Realizing she was stalling, Saura straightened her shoulders and breezed across the room. All she had to do was open the door.

Chapter 12

It wasn't that big of a deal. And yet as Saura reached for the knob, that primal place that had taken over after Adrian's death warned that she was walking into more than just the adjacent room.

"What took you—" John's gruff words died the second their eyes met. Dressed in all black he looked more like a musician than a cop, except his hair was cut far too short. But the hint of a goatee at his chin was right, as was the small gold hoop in his left ear. He'd not been wearing that when he arrived.

And his eyes, the deep olive glimmered with an edginess she'd not seen before, as if all throttles were go, but he wore lead boots that would not let him move.

"John—" she said, because she couldn't just stand there while he watched her as if he expected her to pull a gun any minute and mow him down. "Can you get this for

me?" Lifting the hair from her shoulders, she turned to reveal the zipper caught a few inches below her neck.

A rough sound broke from his throat as she felt his hands, so large and warm against her back. The shiver was immediate, the hazy flash from six weeks before, when he'd put his hands to her body, when he'd undressed her, then made her forget.

Now, dear God, he made her remember.

"Thank you," she said the second she felt the zipper slide into place. Briskly she released her hair and started toward the kitchen. "Nathan should be here soon—"

"*Saura.*"

The sound of her name on his voice slipped like a silken ribbon through her chest, and tightened. She made herself turn, made herself breathe even as she saw him crossing toward her. Sometimes she forgot how big he was, how dominating his presence could be. He was so adept at slipping in and out of the shadows.

All part of the game, she knew. All part of the act. Detective John D'Ambrosia could be anyone, anything. Best friend or worst enemy, junkie or hero, loner or lover. It all depended upon the game, and the role.

Closing in on her, he stopped so close she had to lift her eyes to see his. "Put this on," he said, handing her a small black box she hadn't noticed before.

She took it and lifted the lid, felt her breath catch at the sight of the black cameo.

"For tonight," he said with no inflection, as if he hadn't just given her an exquisite piece of jewelry. She watched him slide a finger beneath the delicate silver chain, and again lifted her hair as he stepped behind her and draped the necklace around her neck. But she did not understand.

They'd parted tersely the night before. Every time they'd spoken today, their words had been careful and measured. From the moment he'd walked into her fake apartment, they'd been treating each other with strained politeness.

That he would give her a necklace—

She wasn't sure what made her look. Curiosity, perhaps. A penchant for self-torture. But as he fumbled with the clasp, she glanced toward the beveled mirror hanging over the sofa, and watched. Lovers, the casual observer would think. Man and woman standing intimately close, his head bowed as he fastened a necklace around her neck. All she had to do was turn, and she would be in his arms.

But Saura saw only strangers. She was tall, but the woman in the mirror, the woman dressed for romance, looked small and vulnerable, fragile, because of the man, the warm possessiveness of his hands against her nape. He towered over her, grim and isolated even as he touched her.

The awkward intimacy whispered through her, driving home the reality that no matter how much she didn't want to, she felt. The roughness of his hands against her shoulders and the warmth of his breath against her skin. She even felt the frustration that coiled through him and the slow burn of desire in his eyes, the unmistakable cost of his restraint.

Most men she knew, when they saw something they wanted, they went after it. But not John. The more he wanted, she realized, the more he denied.

"I can do it." She lifted her hands to his and took the ends of the necklace, brought them together and easily secured the clasp.

She expected him to bark a gruff comment and step away. He didn't. In the mirror she saw his hands smooth her hair into place. Inside, she felt the warmth of his touch the second his palms flattened along her shoulders.

Through the mirror, his eyes found hers. "There's a chip in the pendant—a tracking device."

Of course. It made sense. They had a job to do. Despite the fact he'd be able to hear every word, every breath, between her and Lambert, John wasn't thrilled about using her as bait.

"No matter where you go," he was saying, "as long as you wear the necklace, I'll know."

And he would be there. Listening. Waiting. It would have been easy for the words, the truth behind them, to seduce. Instead they scraped. Because despite the way he kept his hands on her body, it was the cop who spoke, who reviewed the plan of action.

Not the man making a promise.

Relief, she told herself. That's all she could allow herself to feel. She didn't want a man making promises to her. She didn't want promises, period.

Even as she did.

The realization stunned.

"If that makes you feel better," she said, softer than she'd intended.

"Nothing about this makes me feel better," John said, and then he was turning her in his arms, even as he kept his hands on her shoulders. His eyes glowed with an intensity that scorched clear to the bone. "You don't have to do this, you know that, don't you? You don't have to prove yourself to anyone. There's no one keeping score."

"This isn't about keeping score."

"The hell it's not," he said. "Can't you see what you're doing? You've designed this elaborate test for yourself, as if somehow you actually believe your future really depends upon finding Alec's killer."

She stiffened. "He was my friend—"

"You think this is what he would want?" he bit out. "Alec, your friend, one of the only goddamn men I ever knew who opened the door for a woman every damn time? You think he would want you presenting yourself like some kind of offering to Nathan Lambert? A man he despised? You think he would want you to let that man touch you, kiss you—"

"Stop it!" Twisting from his grip, she stepped away. "Are you sure it's Alec you're talking about?" she asked with the same deadly quiet her brother used when moving in for the kill. "Or yourself?"

His nostrils flared. "You'd like that, wouldn't you? That would make it easier, if this was about me and not the fact that when Adrian died, part of you died, too. Do you really think this is the answer? Risking your own life? Do you think that's how—"

Everything about him went still. He stood there dressed in black, with his face set in stone and his eyes staring at her as if seeing her for the first time—and not liking what he saw.

Saura squared her shoulders, but could do nothing about the silence pouring in from all directions, screaming and swirling and damning…

"My God. *Cain was right.*"

The words were soft and horrified, and they pierced her defensiveness like anger never could. "Right about what?"

John studied her. She half expected him to break into the sign of the cross. "That you have a death wish."

She'd been struck before. By a boy in the third grade, a drunk jock in high school who thought he could use force to gain submission, then later, as *Femme de la Nuit,* by a junkie who thought he could teach her a lesson. Each time a hand had been used, and each time there'd been a sting, followed by a bruise. And each time she'd come back swinging with a strike of her own.

Now she only felt the room shift around her.

A death wish.

"Is that what this is all about?" he asked. He moved toward her again, and though she knew she should preserve the distance she'd deliberately put between them, she watched him close in on her. "The bullet that killed your fiancé only wounded you," he said, and despite his proximity, his voice came at her through a chasm of space and time. "And now you need someone else to finish the job."

Slowly, she shook her head. "No," she said. Or maybe she breathed it. "You don't know what you're talking about." Couldn't. Know.

"Don't I?" He lifted a hand to touch her. But she didn't feel. Anything. Anywhere. Not his hand against her face or his leg against hers. Not even inside, where his words kept slicing. "Just think, if something goes wrong and Lambert catches on to you, silences you, then it will be over, won't it?" His hand slid down her neck. "You won't have to feel anymore. You won't have to hurt."

No, she wanted to say. No, she wanted to believe. But the word wouldn't form, and the truth merged with the lie.

"And then," he added so quietly she had to strain to hear him, "you'll be back with the man you love."

"No." This time she found voice, and this time she moved. She lifted a hand and let her thumb slide along his jaw. "That's not how it is." Not anymore. "I don't want—"

The knock at the door jackhammered through her. She felt her eyes widen as she looked up at John, saw the slow burn in his.

Another knock. Followed by a voice. "Dawn?"

But she couldn't look away from John. Couldn't stop touching him. He still had his hand curved around her neck with a possessiveness that made her bleed in places she'd never thought to bleed again.

Never wanted to bleed again.

Another knock. Harder.

"Go," John said, and against the hoarseness of his voice, her throat tightened. He slid his hand to her shoulder and spun her toward the door. "Lambert is waiting."

She didn't want to. God, she didn't want to walk away from him, to Nathan. Not at that moment. She didn't want to let another man touch her, another man—

"Coming…" Because she had to, she crossed to a small table and swept up her purse, headed for the door. But then she turned and John was there. And before she could even lift her face, his mouth was on hers.

"Dawn, darling? Is everything okay?"

John jerked away from her, but his eyes didn't stop glittering. "I'll be listening." His voice was the one that permeated her dreams. "I'll be there."

"I know," she whispered.

And then he was gone, striding to the utility room adjacent to the kitchen.

Feeling a steel come over her, Saura put a hand to the knob and opened the door. "Nathan," she said, accepting both his handful of white orchids, and his kiss to her cheek. "I'm sorry I kept you waiting."

* * *

"You're shivering."

"Just a bit chilly. I didn't realize we'd be outside."

"Here, take my jacket." Silence. A soft brushing sound. "There—better?"

"Yes, much. Thank you."

"No, I am the one who should be thanking you for being such a good sport. I know you were looking forward to the play."

"Things come up. I understand."

So did John. And he'd stake his life on the fact Nathan Lambert did not have a headache. His abrupt decision to bypass the off-Broadway production had nothing to do with how he felt, and everything to do with what he wanted.

"The pool is lovely," Saura said, and from a catering van one block away, John could see them, Saura and Lambert, strolling among the concrete gods that watched over his Roman-inspired pool.

"We can go inside if you like," Lambert surprised John by saying. But then the other shoe dropped. "Or perhaps I can tempt you with a soak in the hot tub."

He could almost hear Saura's startled smile. "I don't have a suit."

John very seriously doubted that mattered to Lambert.

"I keep several on hand," the other man said, "for occasions such as this. Let me—" The words stopped, replaced by the ringing of a cell phone. "I am sorry," he said, as he had four other times throughout the evening. "I need to take this."

"Of course," Saura said. Then silence, and he knew Lambert had walked away to take a call.

Something was so up. "Time to say good-night," he

whispered into a small microphone. Courtesy of modern technology, the receiver was even smaller, tucked into her ear and concealed by thick auburn hair.

"Not yet." Her quiet words confirmed his suspicions— Lambert had moved away. "I saw something in his study. I need to—"

"No." It was as simple as that. "Not tonight."

"Just a little bit longer," she said. "He's…not himself. I really think he doesn't feel good."

Like hell. "Saura, I mean it—"

"Nathan." He hated the way she said the other man's name, all thick and warm and concerned. "Everything okay?"

"Nothing for you to worry about."

"Maybe we should go inside. You look a little…distracted."

John stared into the darkness beyond the utilitarian van, cataloged every reason he should stay exactly where he was and not swing open the van door and—

And put Saura in even more danger.

"Walk with me," Lambert said. Then silence, and again John's imagination supplied what his eyes did not, the sight of Saura in her skimpy black dress with Lambert's white tuxedo jacket hanging from her shoulders, walking through the moonlight. Tucked inside a trail of azaleas, small solar lights led toward a gazebo—

"It's lovely out here," Saura commented, doing as John had instructed and narrating their movements.

"Yes, I suppose it is," Lambert said quietly. "I'm afraid I don't spend much time in the gardens anymore."

Why? That was the right question. John knew that, knew that Saura did, too. Anything to get the man talking, keep him talking, nudge him into lowering his guard. But only silence crackled through the receiver. John clenched his jaw and waited, felt his heart start to pound.

Patience wasn't the problem. When he needed to, he possessed infinite patience. On a stakeout. In an interrogation. When a woman with the saddest eyes he'd ever seen watched him from across a room.

When she lay on top of him, naked and willing and—

Patience wasn't the problem. But stupidity was. Inaction. He'd never been able to sit through horror flicks, didn't know how to sit there in the darkness and wait for the axe to fall or knife to flash, when he saw what was about to happen.

"Nathan?" The edge of concern to Saura's voice made John sit straighter. "What is it? Did I say something to upset you?"

John splayed his hand against the desk bolted into the back of the van, could almost see Saura gazing at Lambert through those amazing melted chocolate eyes of hers. Her hair would be flowing around her face and against her shoulders.

That was her game, he realized. Press through silence, not brute force.

"You?" Lambert finally said. "No. It's just this place. The gardens. I—I've hardly come out here since I learned of my son's death."

John rose from his seat.

"Andrew loved it out here," Lambert went on. "When he was a boy. He would play pirate and bury treasures everywhere." Another beat of silence. "Once the diamond necklace I gave his mother when he was born went missing, and we were quite sure one of the staff had stolen it."

Saura laughed softly. "He didn't—"

"He did. I found it buried at the base of the gazebo."

The walls of the small van closed in on John. He'd wanted Saura to get Lambert talking, but not like this. Not intimately about the son who'd died in Afghanistan. John didn't see the world in stark contrasts of black and white the way Gabe did, but when it came to law enforcement, he'd learned at a brutally early age that it was the shades of gray that got you killed.

The second a cop started seeing a perp as anything other than a criminal—as a son or father or husband, a respected businessman or pillar of the community—the balance of power shifted. All it took was one hazy second and the price could be fatal—the son of a bitch who'd killed his father had been a renowned surgeon, the son of respectable parents, husband of a city councilwoman, father of four children, a deacon in his church.

And John knew, deep in his gut he knew that as his father had entered the pricey house in a pricey neighborhood, he'd let those factors lull him into the complacency that had killed him.

"When your kids are little, you'd do anything for them," Lambert said, and his voice, so sad and haunted, tightened through John. "Then they grow up and you can't do anything at all."

"Nathan," Saura whispered, and goddamn it, John heard the softening in her voice. This time he didn't stop to think or catalog any reasons. He yanked at the door and stepped into the night, started toward the house.

"Saura." He kept his voice low, didn't want to startle her. "He's playing you."

"I know," she stunned the hell out of him by saying. "I know how hard it is to lose someone you love."

John kept walking. He couldn't march up to the door

and ring the bell, he knew that. But he could get closer. He could be ready.

"It's like something inside of you dies, too," she whispered. "But worse because you're still alive. You get up every morning and look into the mirror, see your face staring back at you, but feel nothing. You walk through the day, you do all the right things, but—"

"Nothing is the same," Lambert finished for her.

"No," she agreed. "Not for a long time."

John walked faster.

"And you don't want it to be," she was saying. "You can't bear for it to be. Everyone tells you time heals all wounds, but there's a part of you that doesn't want to heal, doesn't want to live. Because living means feeling and you know that if you feel, you could lose all over again, and this time the bleeding might never stop."

The insight stopped John cold.

"Every survival instinct you have sends you into lock-down—because it goes against human nature to expose yourself like that. To risk."

But she had, damn it. She was. And yet instead of applauding the courage it took to step toward the future, he'd done nothing but goad her.

"But the darkness doesn't stay forever," she whispered. "It can go away. When you least expect it, something changes, and suddenly you find yourself wanting to live again—"

John didn't know why, but damn it, he ran.

"Is that what happened with you, Dawn?" Lambert's voice was disgustingly gentle. Almost tender. And John knew that the son of a bitch was touching her. Maybe her hand. Maybe her face. "Have you reached that point? Do you want to live again?"

John rounded the corner, saw the elegant old house.

"Yes," she whispered, and the word slammed into John, almost made him trip on the tree-root-gnarled sidewalk. "I do. I never expected it, never dreamed it, but I do. *I want to live.*"

Take your hands off her! he wanted to shout, but knew the words would change nothing. In his mind's eye he could see them in the gauzy moonlight, Lambert holding Saura, probably stroking her back or running a hand along her hair. Next he would—

The two quick gunshots stopped John's world.

Chapter 13

John sprinted. "Saura!" he shouted, no longer giving a damn who did or did not hear him. "Saura! Answer me, damn it!"

Nothing. Just the crackle of silence, in the wake of gunfire.

The St. Charles Avenue mansion looked as graceful as always, with the sprawling trees in the front yard, the inviting wraparound porches, and the warm glow of lights from the windows. No movement. No noise. Not even a hint of violence.

Dark possibilities ripped through him, bringing with them a truth that punished. He'd been careless. He should never have let her be alone with the man, no matter how many precautions they took. It could have all been a trap, everything, the phone calls throughout the evening, Lambert's suggestion that they skip the play and return to his house. The walk through the gardens…

Bypassing the front, John took the eight-foot fence at a

dead run, reached the top and vaulted over, landed on the other side with a hard thud. Then he ran some more.

Dim lights played across the Romanesque cabana. "Saura!" There was no movement, no one running from the house. No security personnel or bodyguards. The earpiece, John realized. He'd heard the gunshots as Saura heard them, but at shortly after eleven, the rest of the world continued to watch late-night TV or sleep.

Through the shrubbery he saw the dome of the gazebo, but the path he'd taken wound in the opposite direction. He plowed through the hedge and slapped at the hanging moss, but never slowed. Not even when he saw them lying at the base of the gazebo.

Sleeping. They looked like they were goddamn sleeping.

...something goes wrong and Lambert catches on to you, silences you, then it will all be over. You won't have to feel anymore. You won't have to hurt.

"Saura." Her name was barely more than a whisper. He lunged toward them and dropped to his knees, violated everything he knew about crime scene preservation and rolled Lambert's body from hers.

John knew death. He knew the feel and sound of it, the scent. And without even checking the man's pulse, he knew Lambert was gone.

"Saura, honey," he whispered, crawling toward her. She lay too still, dark hair strewn across her face, arms extended as if she'd tried to break her fall, Lambert's white dinner jacket engulfing her body and smeared with blood.

"I'm here." Swallowing against the horror, John stroked the hair from her face. He was a cop, damn it. A veteran. Crime scenes were nothing new to him. Death and violence, he'd lived them from the time he was a boy.

But this, kneeling over an unmoving Saura, wanting so badly to scoop her body into his arms and run, just freaking run, was new. This was different. And it made something deep inside him want to shake.

Somehow he found training. And somehow he pushed aside the paralysis of a rookie. And he did not let himself shake. He kept one hand to her face as he ran the other along her body, checking for the source of the blood.

Lambert's, he realized the second he spread the jacket from her body. The blast of relief almost felled him. He didn't let it, knew he could not allow himself to feel. That was the credo that kept him alive, kept him sharp. He could not abandon it now.

"Saura," he tried again, and this time her eyelids fluttered. He took her hand and squeezed, leaned over and brushed a kiss along her mouth. "You're okay," he promised. "I'm here."

A soft sound whispered from her throat. *"Étranger."*

The endearment wove through him, piercing everywhere it touched. It was just a word, damn it. But the feel of her mouth moving against his brought an affirmation he'd never imagined possible.

"John."

He lifted a hand to brush the dirt and dried grass from her face. "Just take it easy, honey. No one's going to—"

Slowly her eyes opened. "You're here."

He wasn't sure she'd ever looked more beautiful. "I am."

Her chest rose and fell with increasingly deep breaths. "I don't under— W-what happened…?" He knew the second memory returned. "Oh, God," she rasped. "Is he—"

"Gone," John answered before she could say the word. Horror hollowed out her gaze. "But that doesn't make any sense, not unless…" This time she let the words trail off, and this time John did not supply the unsaid. They both knew.

Unless the gunman had been aiming for Saura, and hit Lambert instead.

"We've got to get you out of here," he said, going from his knees to a squat. "Can you move? Are you hurt? I can carry you—"

"I—I…" The transformation stunned him. One second she lay on the ground like a broken doll. But then everything about her sharpened and she rolled to her knees and pushed to her feet, and *Femme de la Nuit* returned. "I'm okay."

There was no time to savor the sight of her in the moonlight, so goddamn beautifully alive that he could barely breathe. "Then let's go."

She didn't take the hand he offered her. "Go where? The police will be here any minute—" She paused, and he could tell that she listened. To the silence. "Why aren't there sirens?"

The tightness started low. "I haven't called it in yet."

Her eyes clouded. "But—"

"Not now, Saura," he rasped, taking the hand she'd not given him. "Lambert is dead, and you were the only one with him when he went down. I've got to get you out of here before someone realizes their mistake." He used his body to shield hers as he scanned the swarm of trees. "Now do I have to carry you," he asked, looking back at her, "or can you run?"

Maybe it was the edge to his voice, or maybe the reality of his words, but Saura pivoted and started toward the house. The sight should have sent relief pulsing through him: Saura, up and running on her own. But he could find no relief, not until he had her as far from Lambert's world as possible. Hand in hand, he guided her through the gardens to the cabana, up the steps and toward the side fence. "The van is around the corner—"

She yanked her hand from his. "The van? We can't just leave—"

"The hell we can't." He all but growled, hating the way she was looking at him, half in confusion, half in accusation. "Don't tell me *Femme de la Nuit* never slipped into the shadows before the authorities showed up."

Dark hair fell into her face, accentuating the suspicion in her eyes. "But I'm a freelancer. You're a cop."

His chest tightened. The reminder stung. "Saura, please— I'll explain later. Right now I just need you to trust me."

"I do," she said, but did not move, just stared at him with Lambert's bloodstained jacket hanging from her shoulders. "But I was his date, I was with him when it happened. You were around the corner. We can't leave without—"

"*Dawn* was his date." He stepped toward her and took her hand, hated how cold it was. "Not Saura *Robichaud*." He let a beat of silence build between them, let the implications sink deep. If by some miracle Saura's alias remained intact, the second the police arrived, that would change. And the second her real name surfaced, the real trouble would begin.

"And I," he added, hating the bitter taste at the back of his mouth, "am supposed to be on vacation."

Her chin came up. "W-what?"

The truth burned. "Lambert is not mine, Saura. I'm not supposed to be here, either."

Against the night, a siren sounded. "I don't understand," she whispered, for the first time sounding confused and lost and…wounded in a way *he* didn't understand.

"There is no investigation, damn it!" Lambert was too connected, too powerful. He'd pulled too many strings. "Alec's death was ruled an accident."

She backed away from him. "Oh, my God—"

That was a freaking understatement. "We have to go," he said. "Now! If they find you here—"

He didn't need to say who they were, or what they would do. The truth of it registered in her gaze. She ripped from him and ran toward the house.

"Saura!" He lunged after her, caught up with her at the sliding door. "Didn't you hear me?"

She twisted toward him. "You asked me to trust you," she said. "Now I'm asking the same of you." She paused, nearly slayed him with the fire in her eyes. "Wait here."

Then she ran into the house.

He wanted to run after her. Ninety-nine-point-nine times out of a hundred he would have run after her. But she'd asked him to trust her, and in the darkness of a dead man's patio, he realized that he did.

Later, he told himself. Later he would let himself think about all the protocols he was breaking, both those of the force, and those of the man.

She returned less than two minutes later with her flimsy wrap wadded up and tucked under her arm, Lambert's dinner jacket still dwarfing her shoulders.

The sight made his heart slam too damn hard. Without a word he reached for her hand, and without a word, she took his. Together, they disappeared into the night.

"You're pale. Maybe you should lie down and rest."

Saura shook off her cousin's concern. "I'm fine, just a little dizzy." She'd washed the blood off the second she and John had arrived at Gabe's house, but the spinning wouldn't stop.

"Maybe a shower then—"

"No." Then, because she knew Gabe was only trying to help, she aimed for a smile. It had been after midnight when they arrived, but the television had been on, and he'd answered the door on the first knock. "Thank you. I just…need to think."

Needed John to get back. They'd barely been at Gabe's five minutes before John had taken off. Once she would have resented being tucked away like some damsel in distress, but as he'd pressed a hard kiss to her forehead and promised her she was safe, the realization that he was scared for her, that he didn't want her to be alone, had touched her.

Watching her, Gabe ran a hand along the whiskers darkening his jaw. Several days' worth, she guessed, glancing toward the nearly empty bottle of Scotch on the passthrough to the kitchen. And the bottle of prescription pills beside it.

There'd been a time, not that long ago, when Assistant District Attorney Gabriel Fontenot shaved every day.

Frowning, she moved toward the counter and glanced at the small amber bottle, recognized the pain medication. Then she noticed the piece of white paper with what looked to be pieces of newsprint taped against it.

The whisper of unease was immediate, but before she could read the words he was by her side and picking up the page, wadding it into a ball. "Gabe—" She turned toward him, but the look in his eyes stopped her.

Secrets. They shone in his eyes with an intensity that frightened her, as much for the fact he was keeping them, as for the fact that she could tell. Once, her cousin had been renowned for his poker face. His hand could be a flush or a dud; no one would know by the expression on his face or movement of his body. He was that good, a fact which had served him well in the courtroom.

But now, God, now Saura looked at the cousin she'd loved her whole life, but saw only a stranger, a man in faded jeans and a long-sleeved black T-shirt, whiskers at his jaw and secrets in his eyes. "Gabe, honey, what's going on?"

He shoved the crumpled paper into his front pocket and walked into the kitchen. "Nothing you need to worry about," he said. "Just a case I've been working on."

She followed him. "But I thought you were still on leave—"

"I am." He opened the refrigerator and pulled out two bottles of water. "This is personal."

Something about the way he said *personal* jarred her. "Oh, my God—*Camille?*"

He spun toward her. "No. Not Camille."

Her heart kicked hard. She wasn't sure why. "Then—"

"Easy there, Nancy Drew," he said, and just like that the old Gabe was back, the charming lawyer who could disarm with nothing more than a smile. He handed her one of the bottles, and for a crazy minute Saura couldn't help but think, *he knows. Who I am. What I do.* "Don't forget you're the one who came to my door with blood on your hands."

Lambert's blood. Lambert who'd made no secret of his desire to destroy her family. Lambert whom Alec had gone after. Lambert whom she'd targeted, who'd held her hand and talked of a parent's love for a child.

Lambert who now lay dead.

Throat tight, she set down the bottle and lifted her eyes to Gabe's. "There's something you need to see." Something that didn't make sense.

Agitated, she crossed to the kitchen table, where she'd set down her wrap. Unfolding it, she revealed the two files she'd grabbed before leaving, and the small wooden frame.

"What—" Gabe started to ask, but the question died the second he saw the photograph.

John flashed his badge to the patrol officer and strode into Lambert's St. Charles Avenue mansion. Black-and-whites with their lights flashing filled the tree-lined street. An ambulance sat in the driveway, its back doors thrown open. Three news vans were parked across the street.

The reporters were the only ones scurrying. Everyone else moved slowly, methodically. Because everyone else knew running and shouting would change nothing. Nathan Lambert was dead.

If the bullet that took down Lambert had veered a few inches wider…

John strode toward the back of the house. Now was not the time to think of Saura, of the sight of her sprawled beneath Lambert. Now was not the time to think of the way she'd looked at him when she realized he wasn't supposed to be anywhere near Lambert—or the way she'd looked when he'd left her at Gabe's. Thinking of her made everything blur. Thinking of her scraped. Now he had to stay focused. Later—

He didn't know what the hell would happen later.

On the cabana, he looked at the crime scene through the eyes of a cop, saw nothing immediately out of place, only two detectives standing with a grief-stricken Marcel Lambert.

"D'Ambrosia—"

He turned to see a third detective striding toward him. "Glen." A twenty-year veteran, Glen Caves was one of the few men John trusted with his back. "I just heard the report on my scanner." Not entirely a lie. He had flipped his scanner on, and there had been a report.

Glen frowned. "Someone wasted him. One shot, straight through the heart. Coroner thinks he was dead before he hit the ground."

John thought so, too. "Anyone here when it happened?"

"Not when we arrived," Glen said. "No. But the brother talked to Lambert earlier and says he was here with a woman."

John felt himself go very still. "A woman?"

Glen glanced down at the small notebook in his hand. "Dawn, Marcel said. Nathan had been seeing her for a few weeks."

Less than ten feet away, Marcel lowered his face into his hands, and started to sob.

"We've put out an APB," Glen was saying, "but the brother doesn't know her last name or where she lived. He just says there's something off about her, but Nathan refused to see it."

The noose wound tighter, deeper. "Anything else?"

"Not much. His tuxedo jacket is missing, but there's no way to know about anything inside the house yet. He did receive several calls on his cell phone tonight, most from a number registered to a Joe Smith."

The name kicked through John. "Joe Smith?"

"Cute, huh?" Glen scowled. "Oh, and one other…from Francois Hebert."

And after each call, Lambert had been increasingly agitated. Standing there watching the man's brother try to gather himself, John realized his mistake. He'd been seeing the night through the eyes of a jealous lover—not a cop. The jealous lover had seen only a man who wanted to get a beautiful woman in bed. But the cop…

If the cop had been looking, he would have seen a criminal running scared.

Against a gray sky, the three gangly young men stood on a dock, each holding up a string of fish. Their clothes were plain, khaki shorts and knit shirts. It was a nondescript pose in a nondescript place, completely devoid of any telltale sign to pin the picture to a particular decade.

Except for the subjects. In the torn old photograph they couldn't be more than twenty. Now, they were well into their fifties. At least the one who still lived was. One had been gone for almost twenty years. The other, only a few hours.

"What the hell is Uncle Troy doing with the Lambert brothers?" Cain looked up from the picture. He'd arrived less than fifteen minutes before, courtesy of a phone call from John. He knew Lambert was dead. He knew John didn't want Saura left alone. But considering the warm hug he'd given her, she doubted he knew about the blood she'd washed from her hands. "Did you know about this?" he asked Gabe.

Their cousin let out a rough breath. "No."

Cain twisted toward her. "And where did you say this came from? Lambert's house?"

"In his study." She'd seen the picture while waiting for Nathan to take a call, had for a brief moment thought the man in the middle was Gabe. "I—I thought Gabe should see it. Look…" She pointed to the right side of the photograph, where a young Nathan stood. "There was someone else there." A shoulder and pants leg were visible to his left, the face and body torn away. "If we find out who that person is—"

"No."

The edge in her cousin's voice stopped her. Saura looked up, felt the chill in his eyes clear down to her toes.

"The only thing this picture proves," he said very slowly, very carefully, for one fractured heartbeat reminding her desperately of the eloquent attorney he'd once been, "is that Nathan Lambert was an even bigger son of a bitch than we thought." His eyes went cold. *"They were goddamn friends."*

With the finality of a closing argument, he laid the picture face down on the table, then walked into the kitchen, leaving a stunned Saura alone with her brother, and the truth.

It wasn't just a picture she'd given Gabe. Or a lead or a clue, as she'd intended. But in telling her cousin of Lambert's death, she'd given him closure.

"What if it wasn't him?" She looked up at her brother. "What if we were wrong about Nathan Lambert?" For so long she'd allowed herself to see him only as a threat to her family. The man who killed her uncle. But tonight, in those final hazy minutes, there'd been a sorrow in his eyes completely at odds with the monster she believed him to be. "What if he wasn't responsible for Uncle Troy or Alec's death? What if he knew something, and that's why he was killed?"

"Don't."

The sound of John's voice rushed through her. She turned and found him standing inside the front door.

Chapter 14

The sight of John, so tall and isolated, with his dark hair cut brutally short and the hoop in his left ear, did cruel, cruel things to the equilibrium Saura had been trying to find. Everything tilted, blurred.

"Don't start second-guessing yourself." Her heart slammed as he started toward her. "Just because the man loved his son doesn't suddenly turn him into an innocent victim."

"I know." But she didn't know what she saw in John's eyes. They were even more closed than when he'd left almost two hours before. She felt herself move toward him, made herself stop. Now was not the time to reach for him, to feel anything other than cold, rational resolve.

"His son?" Cain came up beside her. "What does he have to do with anything?"

The lines of John's face tightened. "Nothing."

"I'm not so sure," Saura said. "There was something in his eyes." A look she knew well. And for a crazy moment, there in the shadow of the gazebo, she'd forgotten. Everything. Except what it was like to love, and to lose. "It was almost like…fear. When he came back from that last call, I could almost feel the fear coming off him."

A harsh sound broke from John's throat. "You felt what he wanted you to feel," he said. "He was trying to soften you up, keep you off balance." Something indefinable hollowed out his gaze. "The second he could get you to see him as a grieving father, he owned you. From there—"

"No." She stepped closer but did not allow herself to touch. "That's not the way it was."

She would have sworn he winced. But before he could tell her how wrong she was, as he so clearly wanted to do, Cain was there, the hot, burning look in his eyes so murderous she wasn't sure whether to laugh or cry. "Someone want to tell me what the hell's going on here?"

She'd expected anger. She'd expected a lecture. She'd expected her brother to tell her how careless she'd been, to outline every risk she'd taken.

She'd not expected the sadness. She'd not expected Cain to close his eyes, only to open them a moment later and look at her as though she'd just ripped his heart out. He'd said her name—much as he'd sometimes spoken Renee's name, when he thought her investigation into a crime syndicate had gotten her killed. Then he'd said four simple words.

This has to stop.

A full hour later, the memory wouldn't stop needling. Saura let the warm water of John's shower sluice down on her body. He'd barely said a word since insisting Lambert had been playing her. He'd stood aside while Cain took her hand and told her it was time to quit punishing herself. Time to quit playing with fire.

Time to live again.

He didn't understand, she thought, reaching for a well-worn bar of soap. Neither of them did. She knew it was time to live again. That's why she'd gone after Lambert, not because she had a death wish. It was a *life wish* she had, a life wish which had driven her not to protest when John had assured Cain that he would drive her home. He just hadn't specified *whose* home. They'd sped south in his restored Mustang like the strangers they'd never been. Not talking. Not touching.

She'd gotten the sobering impression he didn't trust himself to do either.

Maybe that should have scared her. Maybe she should have insisted he turn around and take her home, rather than let herself step foot in his house. Stand naked in his shower and wash the nonexistent blood from her body.

But that would have been the easy way out, and Saura had never been much on easy. So she rinsed the soap from her body and turned off the water, stepped from the shower and reached for the towel.

It was time to show John the files.

Through the darkness he saw her. She paused across the room, hair tangled and dress torn, her eyes unnaturally dark against a face unnaturally pale. But she didn't move. Didn't say a word. Didn't need to.

John saw, and he felt, and he knew.

On a purely guttural surge of adrenaline, he broke the stillness and kicked out his leg, spun, then struck with his other leg. Higher. Harder. His arms came next, striking with razor precision. Now was not the time for mercy. For distractions. He had to stay sharp, keep his senses alive. All of them. Not just those that fired every time he saw her. Thought of her. The senses that ground through him even now, playing the sound of gunshots over and over, remembering the sight of her lying beneath Lambert.

She wasn't supposed to be there, damn it. Not in his darkness, not in his house. His shower. But even with the bandanna over his eyes, he knew he would find her, exactly where he'd seen her.

Very little surprised John. He'd taught himself to be ready for anything, to walk through each moment without letting it affect him. He'd held the hand of a dying man and absorbed the tears of a grieving mother, he'd walked into darkened buildings and faced a meth-crazed junkie over the barrel of a sawed-off shotgun. But until he ripped the damp cloth from his eyes and saw her standing exactly where he'd known she would be, his breath had never flat-out stopped.

The sight of the hair slicked back from her face, his flannel shirt hanging from her shoulders and her feet bare, fed some place inside of him, some place dark and cold and festering. Pale pink, damn it. Her toenails were painted pale pink.

"The spare room is down the hall," he said, wadding the bandanna into a tight ball. "Second door on the right."

She didn't move. "Trying to get rid of me?" she asked with the whisper of a smile. "You could always take me home, you know."

She'd been in his shower. Naked. Using his soap. Now she wore his clothes. "No."

Her lips, untouched by makeup, curved. But not into a

smile. "No what?" she asked. "No, you're not trying to get rid of me? Or no, you're not going to take me home?"

A sharp twist pierced him. He'd had no choice but to bring her here, into his home, no matter how strongly his professional instincts had objected. He wanted to hate her for that, for forcing his hand and infiltrating his investigation, his life, for tangling their fates so tightly together that he couldn't so much as breathe without it affecting her. This wasn't what he wanted—her standing barefoot in his living room, a few feet and the buttons of his work shirt all that separated them. But he'd never be able to live with himself if he let her go, either.

They would find her. Maybe the cops would get to her first. Or maybe it would be Lambert's assailant. The end result would be the same. The fact that she was a Robichaud wouldn't spare her.

And it would be his fault. His fault because he'd been too damned weak to let her stay.

"They know you were with him," he said, because he had to say something, damn it. Saura Robichaud was not the kind of woman to be led blindly through a minefield. "Lambert's brother told them."

"I have nothing to hide."

"Yes," he said very quietly. "You do."

"The authorities need to know—"

"What? That you were investigating Lambert? That you suspected him in Alec's death? Do you really think that will buy you anything?" The question practically tore out of him. "You're a Robichaud. Your family's contempt for the man is no secret."

Her eyes flashed. "I have proof—"

"You have nothing." For the first time he allowed

himself to move, striding toward the old trunk where he'd left the files. He'd reviewed everything except one disc, which was encrypted. For that, he would need Tara. "Names and dates and places, but nothing signed in Lambert's blood. Nothing to prove it was him."

"You don't know that." Her denial was uncharacteristically soft, almost bruised.

He twisted toward her, felt the punch low in his gut. "Say I'm wrong," he said. "Say there's something on the disc. And the cops know it was you who took it. Then what? You really think whoever killed Lambert is going to let you get away with that?"

He saw the realization come over her.

"Maybe these files can prove Lambert killed Alec," he said, "but at what cost? Lambert is *dead,* Saura. Dead. Someone *killed* him." With her standing only a breath away. "It's only a matter of time before they come after you, too."

She held his gaze for a long moment before looking away, toward the display box mounted on the opposite wall, where his father's badge mocked him.

The urge to smash a fist through the glass stunned him. "I knew better." He ground the words out. "I knew better than to use you like that, to dangle you like bait—"

She spun on him so fast he didn't have a chance to prepare. "You did what I asked you to do," she reminded him, and her eyes practically glittered. "It was a chance I had to take."

Because she didn't care. Because no matter what she said or how strenuously she protested, Saura Robichaud didn't care whether she lived or died.

But he did, damn it. "Just like leaving Lucky's with a stranger." The denouement was flat, a sour conclusion after a marathon interrogation. Everything she'd said, everything she'd done, had simply brought them right back to where they'd started.

There was a calmness to her that had not been there before. "I knew you wouldn't hurt me."

"Are you sure about that?" he asked. "Or maybe it was simply that you wouldn't let yourself feel it if I did?"

Something jagged flashed through the brown of her eyes, but before she could speak, he fired another round. "And Lambert? You still think he wouldn't have hurt you?"

She remained so very, very still, looking at him for the first time as though he was the one with a weapon in his hand.

"No matter what lies you've told yourself," he pressed, "somewhere inside you know the truth. We both do. Lambert wasn't going to let you walk away tonight. He had plans for you."

"And we had plans for him," she reminded.

But he was beyond the point of hearing. "Do you have any idea what it was like?" he asked her. "Sitting in that stupid little van, listening to the two of you? Hearing you laugh and listening to you breathe, knowing that when I heard nothing he was touching you, that his hands or his mouth—"

Now she moved. She eliminated the distance between them, stopping only a motion away from connecting. "Tell me something," she said.

He watched her mouth form the words, reminded himself of all the reasons he could not touch.

"Who is it you don't trust? Me…or yourself?"

The words stung him like acid rain, and all that control, all that rock-solid iron body armor, started to crumble. "I let you go that night for a reason, Saura. If I'd wanted to, I could have stopped you."

Her chin came up a notch. "I know."

But she was still here, damn it. She was still looking up at him as though everything in her world somehow depended on it. "You just don't know when to be afraid, do you?"

Her smile was so damn sad he felt it move through him like a dull knife. "I never said I wasn't afraid."

The admission rocked him. "Do you have any idea," he asked, barely recognizing the rough edges to his own voice. "Any idea at all what it did to me hearing those shots and not knowing? Running and wondering and—"

"I know." The words were so muted everything inside him froze. She cradled his cheek. "I'm here," she said, and somehow the words soothed, even as they blistered. "I'm safe."

"No," he said. "You're not."

But she didn't heed his warning, closed the gap between them, bringing her body against his and pushing up on her toes. "I'll take my chances," she murmured, and then her mouth was on his, gently at first, little damning kisses along his lower lip, at the corners, soft, sweet. Urging. Then stronger. Harder. Her mouth parting, her tongue teasing.

And he couldn't do it anymore, couldn't pretend a part of him hadn't died when he'd heard those shots, couldn't hide that he had gone to his knees when he'd found her unmoving beneath Lambert. From the moment he'd found her pulse, when her eyelids had fluttered, the need to drag her into his arms, to put his mouth to hers and never let her go, had pounded through him. But he'd resisted. He'd tried so damn hard to be the cop, to focus on what needed to be done.

Even if that meant lying.

Even if that meant violating everything he'd always

believed in. He'd tampered with a crime scene. He was with-holding evidence. He was breaking so many rules and laws—

All to keep her safe. Saura. That was all that mattered. Keep her safe, make sure no one found her, hurt her. Not even himself. But the feel of her pressed against him, of her cool, soft hands moving along his arms and around to his back, of her mouth whispering against his, erased everything else. There was only her, and him, and the need that had tortured for six weeks, since the night he'd made love to her, then let her walk away.

On a hard rush he closed his arms around her and tried not to crush, opened his mouth to hers, and quit being a cop.

Sometimes fear punished, and sometimes it paralyzed. But other times it seduced, drawing you to the edge and tempting you to look over, to see what lay on the other side. To wonder. To want. For so long Saura had believed being afraid meant being weak, so she'd elbowed it aside and charged forward, never realizing that to fear was to feel, to be alive.

Now she knew, and now she would not let herself retreat. The quickening was too strong. She'd not expected this, not expected him. When she'd walked into the den and found him in nothing but a pair of sweatpants and a bandanna around his eyes, moving his body with exacting discipline, she'd been certain he was going to shut her out.

She'd been wrong.

He crushed her in his arms, the struggle that defined him played out in his kiss. Desire clashed with restraint, hot and greedy, but tragically gentle, sensuous, as if he wanted to savor every broken second. Every sigh. Every taste. His mouth moved against hers stronger, more demanding. His arms held her close, while his hands roamed her back and tangled in her hair.

She shifted, loving the way his hands caressed her body, the thick ridge pressing into her abdomen. Pulling back, he looked down at her, his eyes glittering with that impossible combination of need and restraint. Valiant down to his last, bitter stand, she realized faintly, and her heart did a long free fall through her chest.

"Do you know what happens to dynamite," he asked, "when the fuse has been burning slowly…" Sliding his thumb to her lower lip, he rubbed. Very slowly. Very softly. "Sizzling…" Lowering his face to hers, he kissed his way along her jaw to her ear. "Charring its way toward the lonely stick?"

A sizzling fire ignited within her. "Tell me."

"There's a point of no return." His voice was so hoarse she had to concentrate to hear him, concentrate not to lose herself in the feel of his hands and his mouth drifting across her face. "A point past which there's no turning back."

"And then what happens?" she asked, wondering who this man was who could speak like a poet but look at her as if she held a weapon in her hands.

"A smart person runs."

But he hadn't moved a muscle. "You mean a coward."

His eyes burned brighter.

It was her turn to lift a hand to his face, her turn to touch, to skim a finger along the cleft in his chin. "And a brave person?" she whispered. "What would a brave person do?"

Deliberately he slid his hand from her face down along her neck, lower to her collarbone. There he rubbed. "Depends upon his goal. He might try like hell to defuse it."

As he'd done. As he'd been doing from the start.

But now the look in his eyes, the hunger and the tenderness, seduced with a completeness that made her chest go tight. "It's too late for that." It had been too late for a long, long time.

His slow smile stole what remained of her breath. "Then it looks like the poor bastard's going up in smoke."

She wasn't sure how she stayed standing. "Show me." Need drove her. She slid her hands from his face to his shoulders, then down along the tightly corded muscles of his shoulder and back. "Show me."

"You have no idea…" With his mouth, he traced the path of his hand, sliding his lips along her jaw, her neck, her collarbone. "I tried," he said, "to forget you, to forget this. But you were always there, and all I could think was how it felt to touch you." He looked up and met her eyes. "Taste you."

The quickening started low, spread fast. "Tell me how," she whispered, and his eyes took on a dark glow.

"Like more."

He picked her up then, body to body. She wrapped her bare legs around his equally bare waist and aligned her mouth with his. From outside she heard the wind blowing through the trees and against the window. Cold. But in here there was only warmth, heat, the absolution of John's kiss and the restrained power of his body as he walked with her wrapped around him toward his bedroom.

With her legs curled around his waist and her arms circling his neck, she held on, didn't ever want to let go.

The truth stunned her. Until six weeks ago, when she'd looked into the eyes of a stranger and felt the first fissures of a thaw, there had been nothing. Now as he set her on a bed as Spartan as the one that first night, it was a rush to feel more that had her pulling him down with her. She ran her hands down the firmness of his stomach to his waist-band, then slipped inside and found him, thick and long and jutting up amidst the coarse hair. The feel of him thrilled, unleashing a yearning, spreading slowly, languidly, like the warmest, sweetest of honeys.

"Show me…" She feathered the words along his chest, finding a flat mauve nipple to tease with her tongue. Then to encircle with her mouth, and pull.

His answering sound spurred her on, and in some hazy corner she realized the fear was gone. The caution. There was only desire, nudging her toward that hazy place where dreams and reality collided, and the future was born.

"Saura," he whispered as he'd not done that first night, when they'd shared their bodies, but not their names. When she'd naively thought she could take this man once, and not crave him for the rest of her life. Not feel him, not need him.

"You were wrong."

Her heart stuttered hard on the words. She raised her head and met his eyes.

"Last night," he said. "About before…the night at Lucky's."

Somehow she breathed.

"I didn't see a lonely woman." The feel of his thumb, skimming her cheekbone, destroyed. "I saw a beautiful woman," he stunned her by saying, "a woman who did the impossible…who made me feel alive."

An inner fortification completely gave way. She blinked against sudden tears, but could do nothing about the emotion cresting through her.

"You don't know, do you?" he asked, lifting a thumb to swipe at the single tear, just as he'd done the night in the swamp. Then he placed a soft kiss where the moisture had been and lowered his hands to her shirt. There he thumbed the buttons, until the flannel fell open and nothing remained between them except her panties and his sweats. "You don't know what you do to me."

But she wanted to. "Show me." On the verge of shattering she reached for his waistband and shoved, baring the bulge beneath the gray cotton of his boxer briefs.

The sight sent a dark thrill twirling through her.

Not wanting to wait, she curved her hands around his neck and urged him down, taking his mouth with hers. He let out a guttural moan, then took over the kiss and made it his.

He made everything else his, as well. With his hands he claimed her body; with his gentleness he took her heart. She twisted beneath him, holding him to her, straining to touch as much of him as she could. Before long they shed their underwear and nothing remained to separate flesh from flesh.

His mouth was everywhere, kissing, licking, sucking. Just like that first night, hot and seeking, hungry. But different somehow, slower, more intimate. He skirted along the edge of one nipple, tracing small circles, flicking his tongue along the peak. Need arced through her; pleasure bordered on torture.

The fuse, she knew, had almost reached the stick.

She urged him fully on top of her, and when she felt the weight of him against her, she let her legs fall open in welcome. She loved the feel of him between her thighs, all hard and solid, pressed against her.

She writhed, needed him inside.

But instead he lifted his head and met her gaze, slid a hand to cup her face. "I don't want to hurt you."

The restraint in his voice heightened the urgency to have him inside her, again. And again.

"The only way you could hurt me, would be to stop." She wrapped her legs around his and tilted her hips forward. "Please," she said on a soft breath. "Don't stop."

She saw him swallow, saw his throat constrict with the movement. The look on his face, an expression bordering on pain, ripped at her. "Now," she urged again. "Please."

"My name." His hand found hers and held. "Say my name."

The request thrummed through her, made everything inside of her go soft and warm and liquid. "John," she whispered, loving the sound of his name on her lips, aware of how rarely she'd used it. Another self-imposed barrier, she realized, and vowed to shatter them all. *"John."*

With his free hand he brushed the hair from her face. "I want to see you," he murmured, then pushed inside. For a moment there was stillness as she took him and held him, adjusted to his width. Then her body relaxed and he started to move. She moved with him, lifting her hips and welcoming him, running her hands along his back and holding him as close as she could.

"I want to see you, too." Throat tight she watched him, drank in the look on his face as he pulled out and thrust back inside, deeper each time, long, sensuous strokes.

Raw desire had punctuated that first night, but now it was something even more basic that fueled them. Now it was need. Not for a stranger, but for him. For John. And the future he'd made her see. It bled through her like an electric current, destroying the restraint and the caution. The fear.

The point of no return, she thought hazily.

Closing her eyes, she savored the sensation of him moving inside her as if he wanted each second, each stroke, to last an eternity. The fire and the wonder, the salvation she'd never expected to find, washed through her.

"Please," she whispered. "John…"

He opened his eyes and gazed down at her through eyes glazed by passion.

"Up in smoke," he murmured as he pulled out, then plunged back in for one last deep thrust before the world exploded around them.

The bedroom window rattled against the wind. John nestled Saura closer, pulled the sheet up to cover her back. Silently she relaxed into him and let out a soft breath. Unlike him, she slept. She sprawled over him, her head on his chest and her hair feathering against his flesh, her arm over his abdomen and a leg slung over his. He couldn't stop running his hands along the soft warmth of her body. Couldn't let his eyes drift shut, didn't trust himself to drop off.

The last time he'd done so, she'd slipped from his arms and out of his life.

He could have stopped her. He knew that. He'd awakened the second she rose from his bed, had felt the slow incursion of the cold as he'd lain there and listened to her dress. To her breathe. To what he would have sworn was a soft sob.

Then he'd listened to her walk out the door.

He could have stopped her.

Now he held her, stared up at the slow-moving blades of his ceiling fan and breathed deep and steady. Slowly. Consciously.

If he let it, contentment could creep in with vicious ease.

The cop he'd always wanted to be rebelled at the thought, and for a change, the man agreed. Contentment led to complacency, and complacency made a man weak.

Death had many faces, he knew. Some of them more appealing than others. But all equally destructive.

He closed his eyes, felt his chest tighten beneath the whisper of her breath.

Too easily he could see her as she'd been that first night, when he'd sat nursing a drink and pretending not to notice. Pretending not to see. Six days later, the night after he let her walk away, he returned to Lucky's. But she hadn't been there. He'd told himself it was just as well, that he'd let her go for a reason, but he'd asked the waitress about her anyway.

She won't be back, the waitress had said. *That one prefers the shadows.*

The shadows? Why's that?

No one can see her then. No one can hurt her.

The words haunted. All along, the man he was had resisted what the cop saw. The vulnerability. The fear. The hope. That's why he'd let her go. But now—

She shifted against him, and her eyes opened against the darkness. "John…"

His name, damn it. That was all he'd asked for, for her to say his name. Now the sound of it on her sleepy voice tormented him. "I'm here," he said, against a throat ridiculously tight. "Go back to sleep."

She blinked up at him, ran her hand along his chest. "You're real."

Simple words, but they scraped to the bone.

Her smile was soft, trusting. "You're usually gone when I open my eyes."

Somehow, he didn't wince. But nor did he say the words that whispered through him. *I'm not going anywhere.* "Then maybe you should keep your eyes shut," he murmured. He wanted to taste her again, damn it. Again and again and again.

For a long moment she said nothing, just watched him through those amazing eyes that had once been so lost, but now shone with a contentment he'd never imagined possible. Not from her. Then she lowered her face to his and kissed him, not hard and hungry like before, but sweet and lingering.

Then she pulled back. "Why didn't you tell me you were on leave?"

Everything inside of him tensed. Defenses flexed, but when he looked at the light in her eyes, he realized she wasn't moving in for the kill or interrogating, she was simply a woman asking her lover a question.

He was the one imagining the noose around his neck. "It wouldn't have changed anything."

"I would have understood," she said. "I know about needing to do things that everyone thinks you shouldn't."

He closed his eyes against the words, against her, but they both waited for his response. "I've violated so many rules I don't even recognize myself anymore." He bit the words out, opening his eyes.

Saura's smile was soft. Her touch was gentle. "*I'm* the one who took the files," she reminded.

But tampering with a crime scene was only the tip of the iceberg. "I didn't stop you. I—"

She slid over him and cupped his face. "What?" she asked, her hair falling against his neck. "You what?"

He wanted to tell her. God, so much.

But he didn't know how.

"All I could do," he said, closing his arms around her, "all I could think about," he added, "was getting you out of there." Getting her safe. "And doing this," he rasped, urging her face to his.

Then he let his actions speak for him.

The phone woke him. John came awake hard, sat up and felt the punch clear down to his soul.

She was still there.

Through the murky light of early morning he saw her sleeping on her side, curled slightly, dark hair spilling against his pillow and the sheet pulled over her body.

Then the phone rang again, and she stirred.

Heart thumping, he forced himself to turn from her and grab his handset from the nightstand. "D'Ambrosia."

Silence.

"Hello?" he barked. "Who's this?"

"A-are you," came a voice so low he had to strain to hear her, "the cop?"

He sat up a little straighter. "I am. Who's this?"

"I—I…know things," she said as Saura came up behind him and draped her body around his. "A-about the Lamberts."

"Who is this?" he asked again. "How did you get my number?"

"You…don't know me," she said. "But I've heard your name. They talk about you."

Saura let out a soft breath.

"I—I'm scared."

"Tell me where you are." Pulling away from Saura, he stood and reached for his pants. "I can meet you, we can talk—"

"No, if he finds out—"

"I'll protect you," he said, reaching for his shirt. "Nothing's going to happen to you. Just tell me where you are."

* * *

She watched him go.

It was an odd thought, Saura knew that, but as she saw John holster his Glock, she knew the man who'd loved her through the night was gone. It was the cop who agreed upon a meeting spot with the caller, who barked out instructions.

And it was the cop who turned to Saura after disconnecting the call. "I have to go."

"I know."

But he didn't move, surprised her by hesitating. "Does the name Darci mean anything to you?"

No, she started to say, but then the memory clicked. "Maybe," she said, slipping from the bed. Against the cool morning air she reached for his flannel shirt. "At the party," she said, sliding an arm into a sleeve. "There was a girl looking for Marcel…"

"Do you know anything about her?"

"No, we talked briefly, I—"

John's eyes went wild. "Get down!" he shouted, lunging, but the window shattered with his words. The pain was immediate. She felt herself stagger, felt John catch her.

Then everything just stopped.

Chapter 15

"Saura!"

He rolled from her and slid an arm around her waist, dragged her away from the window. On the other side of the bed he grabbed his Glock and held it ready as he crouched over her.

The blood on his hand turned everything inside him horrifically cold. It was not his own.

"Sweetheart," he said, more desperately this time. His heart slammed hard and quick. He had two rounds. He could hold the shooter at bay. But if there were more of them— If they came at him from multiple directions— If someone burst through his door as another came up at the window—

He would have to leave her. He could not tend to her and stave off an attack at the same time. He had more ammo in his closet. He could—

Silence. The clarity of it struck him. He hated to look

away from her, but had to. Sun poured in through the blown-out window, but he no longer saw the glint of a shotgun.

"*John.*"

The sound of his name kicked through him. He turned back and found her watching him through eyes so glassy something inside twisted.

"I—I'm okay," she said.

He swallowed hard. "Tell me where you hurt." But even as he ran his hands along her body, he couldn't stop watching. Stop listening. "You're bleeding."

"The glass—" she struggled to sit "—not the gun. It's just cuts."

For a sweet moment the tightness inside him released, and he tucked her into his lap and rocked her against him, felt his throat go tight when she curled her arms around his waist.

The simple gesture slayed him.

Beneath his bloodstained shirt she was still warm and soft and naked, but as John stared toward the window, as he kept his Glock pointed and his finger on the trigger, he felt neither warmth nor softness. Only nakedness. More naked than he'd ever allowed himself to be.

And that's when the tightness returned.

"This isn't the way to New Orleans."

John steered the old Mustang out of a right turn and picked up speed, but neither confirmed nor denied Saura's observation. Dark sunglasses hid his eyes, but she could tell that he checked the rearview mirror. He had one hand on the wheel, the other in his lap. Next to it lay his Glock.

He'd been this way ever since easing her from his lap and instructing her to get dressed. His eyes had been grim, a grimness that seeped more deeply through her with every silent breath he took.

She'd assumed they were going to the city to meet up with Darci. But they traveled west, not east. And as the oak and cypress and pine raced by in a blur of brown and green—and minutes dragged into miles—she realized John and the girl must have agreed to meet somewhere else.

The second he turned down the partially concealed dirt road, the thoughts blurred. Her throat tightened as she saw the grand old house in the distance, barely visible through naked tree branches. During the spring and summer, when foliage was at its peak, a passerby would never know the house was there.

But then, no one just passed by the Robichaud ancestral home. Ridiculously secluded, the gothic estate had stood for over a hundred years, sheltering and guarding.

It was the perfect place for a secure meeting.

Slowing, John turned into the circular drive and stopped next to Cain's convertible. Just ahead she saw two other cars—those belonging to Renee and Uncle Edouard—but no sign of the girl Darci.

"What time is the meeting?" she asked, glancing toward John.

He slid the gearshift into park. "In thirty minutes."

"Good, that gives us a little time to—" She wasn't sure why she broke off. Maybe because he'd made no move to turn off the engine. Or maybe because he'd made no move, period. Not to look at her. Not to reach for the door. He simply…sat there. "John?"

Against the steering wheel, his hand tightened, and slowly, he faced her. "Cain's waiting for you."

She felt herself go very still. "For *me*," she said with a

quietness that had nothing to do with anything soft or tender. Because she knew. *For her.* Her brother was waiting for her. Not them. "Darci's not coming here," she whispered.

The muscle in the hollow of his cheek thumped. "No."

Just *no.* Somehow she breathed, even as her throat constricted and everything flashed a thousand shades of stark, brutal white. It all made sense. Everything. The near unbearable silence of the car ride. The way he'd quit looking at her. Quit touching.

And something inside her snapped. She moved so fast he had no time to block her, no time to stop her from yanking the sunglasses from his face.

What she saw almost made her want to put them back on.

Nothing. She saw absolutely nothing in his eyes. No warmth. No tenderness. No pain or hurt or struggle. Nothing.

Deep inside, something fragile and beautiful, something she'd never imagined she would feel again, want again, simply shattered. But when she spoke, her voice was calm. "You're not coming back, are you?"

His eyes went hard. "I'm a cop. I have a job to do."

She looked at him, looked for one trace of the man from the night before. Saw only the *étranger* she'd once thought she could have without wanting. Love without loving. "And that's what it all comes down to, isn't it?" Hearing the hurt creep in, she stripped it from her voice. But could do nothing for her heart. "You're a cop—but what about the man?" For emphasis she paused. "John." Again she waited, looking for a wince or a flicker, anything. "Isn't that what you asked for last night? For me to say your name, not your rank?"

She saw him swallow, saw his throat work, but he said nothing, just watched her as if she were a witness giving him a statement about a petty crime.

"Who was it?" she asked, as she should have done many times before. "Who was it that died and took you with him?" Her heart pounded on the question, the realization. "Who was it that died and turned you into such a coward?"

The planes of his face tightened. His mouth flattened into a hard line. He glanced at the dashboard, then back at her. "I need to go."

The words struck her as pathetically prophetic. He needed to go. To run. Because he didn't know how to stay. Didn't want to try. "You accused me of having a death wish," she said, "but you're the one so dead inside you don't even feel it when the knife you lift is to your own heart."

Now he winced. And now the olive of his eyes took on a dark glitter. "Isn't that what you wanted?" The question was slow, emotionless. "Isn't that why you picked me to begin with? Because you knew I wouldn't care if you walked away? That I wouldn't stop you?"

The ice-cold questions sliced with brutality. She felt herself go very still, felt those fragile places inside start to bleed.

"Yes," she said. "It is."

Never looking away from her, he took the sunglasses from her hands and slid them back over his eyes.

"You're going to do it, aren't you?" she asked. "You're just going to let me walk away."

He put his hand to the gearshift. "I never asked you to stay."

"No, you didn't," she said softly. She was not going to cry. And she was not going to break. Not again.

Because it was the only thing to do, she opened the door and, once again, walked away.

And once again, he made no move to stop her.

* * *

"Darci?"

John knocked a second time, harder. He'd waited for over an hour at the Broad Street library, in the children's section, just as they'd discussed. He'd worn the L.S.U. baseball cap, and he'd held the book about dinosaurs at bedtime in his hands. But no one had approached him. There'd been one young woman cruising through chapter books, but when he'd approached her, she'd made it clear she was not there for him. And the voice had been wrong.

Now he stood outside a small apartment near the Tulane campus. He'd traced Darci's call to her cell phone, from which he'd secured registration information.

"Darci," he called again. A car sat in the driveway. He was having the plates run to see if it was hers. But no one answered the door, despite the soaring music of a soap opera leaking through the thin walls.

He should leave, he knew that. Just as he knew better than to let himself remember the pained look in Saura's eyes when she'd realized he wasn't coming back. That he was letting her go. He'd wanted so damn bad—

He'd wanted. That was the problem. He'd wanted, and he'd taken, and in doing so he'd violated the cardinal rule by which he lived his life.

Frowning, he stepped away from the door, but abruptly spun back and put his hand to the knob, and turned. He crossed the threshold and glanced at the lock, saw that it had to be locked from the inside—or with a key. Which meant—

"Darci!"

A cop learned to trust his instincts, and John's were screaming. He ran through the front room toward the bedroom. And saw her. Lying in bed. Face down. Before he even reached her, he knew she was dead.

This time he called it in. And this time he stayed. He was still waiting for the black-and-white when his cell phone rang. He reached for it, saw the name in the caller ID window: Francois Hebert.

It meant nothing to him. At first. But then the memory sliced in and he jabbed the talk button. "D'Ambrosia."

"Detective," came a voice belonging to a woman, not a man. "This is Violet Hebert." Recognition made him go very still. The old woman he'd interviewed the day before, the one who'd been spotted leaving the warehouse after it exploded, who'd admonished her cat as John had tried to pull information from her. Her cat named Francois.

Francois Hebert. The name of one of Nathan Lambert's final callers.

"I—I've remembered something."

"You sure I can't talk you into coming? I'm sure Mimi can fit you in…"

Saura watched Renee slide her purse over her shoulder. A pedicure sounded heavenly, but if she spent one second longer with her old friend, Renee would see. And if Renee saw, she might reach out. And if she reached out, if she put her arms around Saura…

It stunned her how badly she wanted that. For so long she'd insisted to herself that she didn't want to reconnect with anyone. Now, she realized that she did. Because of John. Because he'd shown her, through harsh brutal example, what happened when someone walked through life without living.

"Next time," Saura said with a smile that was surprisingly unforced. Inside she hurt, but that only meant that she lived.

And loved.

As Renee drove away, Saura wandered behind the house, to where the gardens tapered into a copse of oak and cypress. As a child, the lore of the area had fueled her imagination. She and Cami had searched for buried treasures, those of the Old South and the pirates, a legendary stained glass window smuggled out of France hundreds of years before. They'd been so innocent…

Now she walked the familiar path and breathed the familiar air, and for the first time since John had driven away, she didn't stop the moisture burning her eyes. Instead she put her forehead to the solid trunk of an oak, and allowed herself to remember. To feel. Everything. Not just those broken moments in his car when she'd realized her plan for reclaiming her life had worked beautifully, even as it backfired, but further back. To the look in his eyes when she'd come to after the gunshots to find him hovering over her. To the way he'd touched her before Lambert had picked her up. The way he'd kissed her. To so many other moments, when he'd touched her and made her want. Made her feel.

Standing in the cool dampness of early February, with decomposed leaves at her feet and centuries-old trees towering against a whitewashed sky, she could see him as he'd been that first night, when he'd sat in the back of Lucky's wearing his olive shirt and camouflage pants, nursing a drink he never drank and watching her as a cop on a stakeout might watch a suspect.

The soft crunch came from behind her. A stick, she realized, turning with her brother's name on her lips. He'd always loved to see how close he could get before she heard.

The sight of the gun stopped her cold.

* * *

It could be an ambush. John knew that. He'd suggested a neutral meeting spot, but Violet had insisted on her house. That it wasn't safe to be seen together in public. That he come alone.

Kevlar in place, he lifted his hand and knocked. Cain waited, hidden, at the back of the house.

The door opened and Violet glanced nervously beyond him, toward the sleepy street, empty except for two parked cars, which had also been there the day before.

"Come in," she said. "Quick."

His instincts were in overdrive now, a hard pounding of blood through his veins. He did as she instructed, was barely inside before she closed the door and fastened a series of chains and bolts. He'd noticed them the day before, had attributed them to protection. Now he wondered just who the hell this woman sought to keep out. And why she'd called Nathan Lambert.

"Mrs. Hebert," he started. "You sounded frightened. Has someone else come here? Is someone threatening—"

She glanced from him toward a crack in the brocade curtains. "You sure no one followed you?"

"We're safe," he assured her.

Her eyes, still oddly bright, met his. "Then follow me."

There was a manual full of reasons why he shouldn't, especially when they reached the shadowy hallway with its four closed doors. Cain waited just outside. All John had to do was give the signal and the house would be entered from all directions. Whoever waited behind those closed doors wouldn't stand a chance.

Quietly, John unholstered his Glock.

Halfway down the hall, with her hand on an old glass

knob, Mrs. Hebert glanced back at him. "Aren't you—"
With long silver hair falling into her face, her eyes widened. "What's that for?"

But then the door opened, and as John heard Cain enter through the kitchen, he lifted his gun.

And forgot to breathe.

"Do exactly as I say and this won't hurt any more than it has to."

Until John, Saura had felt nothing. With his hard eyes and gentle hands he'd freed something inside her, and the floodwaters moved through her and she felt. Everything.

She didn't want to go back to the empty cocoon that muted every color, every sound. Every sensation. She wanted to see and hear and taste, to feel. The good, and the bad.

She wanted to live.

That's what gave her the strength to keep her thoughts sharp, despite the 9mm pressed into the small of her back. Forcing the icy numbness that had once defined her world, Saura opened the door and walked inside the sterile apartment she'd last stood in the night before, when John had fastened a necklace around her neck and promised to be listening, watching.

Now he did neither.

Behind her the door closed and the bolt clicked into place.

Working hard to keep her breath steady, she turned to face the man with the soft black hair and empty gray eyes. The last time she'd seen him he'd been posing as a waiter, and he'd smiled at her. Now he wore a black turtleneck and pants, and there were no smiles.

He'd closed in on her like a predator and leveled the gun at her heart, told her to walk. That if she did as instructed, the men with guns trained on her family—on Cain and Renee and Gabe, on her Uncle Edouard—would not be told to shoot. That she would see her lover again.

"Now what?" she asked.

With the gun he gestured her deeper into the apartment. "Now you give me the folder."

The folder. She swallowed hard, kept her chin at a fierce angle. "What folder?"

He stepped closer. "Are we really going to do this, Saura? Play games? Pretend we don't know what's going on here?"

The cool condescension in his voice sent a chill through her. "I'm not pretending."

"Then give me the files you took from my father—now."

Father. The word reverberated through her, sent her heart into a frenetic rhythm. "Your *father?*"

"Nathan Lambert," he said in a voice so hatefully quiet it seemed like venom. "The man you killed."

The room started to spin. Slowly at first, a blur of white with slashes of red and black. Then faster. Louder. "No," she whispered. No, she didn't kill Nathan. No, this man with the dead eyes couldn't be his son. Andrew was...dead.

"That's right," he said, smiling now, much as he'd smiled that night at the party, with the cool confidence of someone who knew how to get what he wanted. "What is it they say about the sins of the father?"

She shook her head, stepped back. "I didn't kill him."

"No?" His eyes glittered. "You were there, weren't you? Using him, lying to him. Standing next to him." He stepped closer. "Don't tell me you really think those bullets were meant for *him.*"

The horror of it stabbed through her. And in the dark corners of her mind she could see it all again: Nathan standing by her side; staring into the night; his eyes going wide and the abrupt movement toward her, the way he'd put his body in front of hers… "My God…"

"Ironic, isn't it?" Something sinister flashed through Andrew's eyes, eyes so very like his father's. But different somehow. Lacking something. "Having your life saved by the man you were trying to destroy."

Ironic wasn't the word she would choose. "A life for a life." The statement barely squeezed through the tightness of her throat. "Is that what this is about?"

"The file," he said. "It's about the file."

And finally she knew. Finally she realized. All along they'd thought it odd that Lambert's activities would suddenly escalate. Escalation wasn't the M.O. of a man nearing retirement. But now all the pieces fell into place, creating a picture they'd never anticipated. Nathan wasn't the one delving deeper into the black market, ferrying young girls and drugs and guns, substandard pharmaceuticals, into the country. It was his son. Andrew was the one escalating. And Nathan, the father, had been the one poised to take the fall.

Then they grow up, and you can't do anything at all…

"I'm not going to let you blow this for me," Andrew said. His voice held no emotion whatsoever. "Just like I didn't let that cop friend of yours stop me."

Alec. The truth stabbed through her. He'd known. He'd found out. "I don't have the file," she whispered.

Andrew moved so fast she had no time to brace herself. "Then you'd better find a way to get it."

The phone clipped to John's belt vibrated, but he made no move for the distraction.

Mike D'Ambrosia's mistake had been to relax. John's father had been lulled into a sense of security by a posh neighborhood and a well-furnished house, a deceptive smile. He'd let down his guard, and he'd died.

John had heard his mother cry herself to sleep night after night. And then as months turned into years, he'd heard other sounds from her bedroom, laughter and the creak of a mattress, thumps against the wall and animalistic sounds he hadn't been able to identify until he'd gotten older. And as the boy he'd been turned into the man, and his mother's desperation again turned to sobs, he'd made a vow to never be caught off guard. To never relax, never let his senses dull to the point where he didn't see what was in front of him and behind him. Beside him.

And for almost twenty years, he'd been successful.

His mistake, John now realized, was to believe that if he lived without living, if he kept his guard hammered into place, he'd never be caught by surprise. He'd never falter, never stumble, never stare at anything he hadn't seen coming.

He hadn't seen this coming. He stood in the small pink room with his back against the wall and his Glock in his hand. He wanted to be angry. Goddamn it, he wanted to be furious. To ground himself in the hot sting of betrayal. He'd been deceived. He'd been misled. He'd been driven to his freaking knees by a guilt that grew and festered with each passing day.

All because of a lie.

But as he swallowed against the hard grind of his throat, he realized that not all surprises destroyed.

"I don't remember much," the grizzled man was saying. *Alec. Sweet Christ have mercy, Alec.* It was a vagrant who'd been burned beyond recognition in the explosion, a vagrant who lay in the crypt outside of town.

Once cool and urbane, the son of privilege who could coerce as easily as he could seduce, now looked like a son of the swamp. His dark brown hair was long, unevenly cut. A full beard covered his jaw. Scars streaked along one side of his neck, and another along his temple. And his eyes, there were shadows there. Secrets. "Vi found me, says I was barely lucid, but I made it clear that if she turned me over to the authorities, I was a dead man. Somehow she got me here and cared for me, didn't let me die."

Sitting on the edge of a twin sleigh bed with a patchwork quilt, Alec glanced toward Cain, standing stock-still in the doorway. "It was only later that I found out why she was there, that she'd lost her youngest daughter to black-market heroin and had found an address among her things, and a name."

John swore softly. "Lambert."

"And the warehouse," Alec confirmed.

Cain crossed to the small window and nudged aside the room-darkening shade.

The phone vibrated again—this time John switched it off.

"I couldn't let anyone know." Dressed in an old red-and-gray flannel shirt, Alec looked about fifteen years older than the last time John had seen him. "If he found out I survived…he would have stopped at nothing to lure me into the open."

"Tara," John muttered. God, Alec's wife.

Something sharp and volatile flashed through Alec's eyes. "I was already dead to her. The explosion didn't change a thing."

John wasn't so sure of that, but now wasn't the time.

"Why now?" Cain strode from the window and squatted in front of his former partner. "Why make contact now?"

Alec grabbed a manila folder from the pillow and shoved it at Cain. "Because of Saura."

Everything inside John stilled.

"Saura—" Cain barked.

Alec stood, suddenly looked like a caged animal. "I tried to stop her," he said, "tried to warn her, but she didn't listen. She didn't understand." He took the file from Cain and opened it, pulled out several pictures. "Now she's in his path." Alec lined up the series of shots on the quilt. "He's escalating, spinning out of control—"

"Alec." The relief was immediate. John stepped forward and put a hand to his friend's forearm. "He's dead."

Alec spun on him, his eyes wild. "Not Nathan," he said. "The son. Andrew."

Everything tilted. John swung toward the pictures, saw the younger, slightly rougher version of Nathan, the son who'd allegedly been killed in the line of duty.

He recognized the girl, the young Russian who'd been found running naked in the Quarter. In this picture she was dressed in a pair of gold pajamas with terror in her eyes. In the next she lay sprawled on the floor, with a man towering over her.

"He's dangerous," Alec was saying. "Greedy. Makes his father look petty in comparison."

Cain already had his cell phone in hand. "You think he killed him?"

"It's possible," Alec said. "Andrew thought his dad thought too small, didn't see the possibilities."

But John did. And he knew. The escalation in black-market activities—not the father, but the son.

"Identity theft, computer viruses, black-market pharmaceuticals…it's just the beginning," Alec said. "If there's a market, Andrew wants to serve it."

"She's not answering," Cain said, and something inside of John stopped. Against the sudden vacuum he grabbed his phone and stabbed it on, fumbled with the small keys until he could see the recent calls. Two of them. Both from the same unlisted number.

Then he saw the symbol indicating a voice-mail message.

"Be okay," he muttered, not giving a damn at the way Cain and Alec stared at him. "Be the hell okay," he growled, stabbing at the keys until he got the message to play.

"John." Saura. Sweet God. The sound of her voice went through him on a hard rush. "About tonight. I wanted to let you know I decided to come back to the city after all— Cain brought me back to my apartment."

His heart stopped. His eyes met Cain's.

"I was hoping you wouldn't mind bringing the file over here," she said with a breeziness completely at odds with the last time he'd seen her— When he'd let her walk away.

When he'd wanted nothing more than for her to stay.

"We can get pizza or something…"

Chapter 16

He could be anywhere. Still with Darci. Back at his house with a bandanna over his eyes, forcing his body through a disciplined tae kwon do routine. His phone could be turned off. He wasn't on active duty after all. And he'd told her goodbye. There was no reason for him to check messages—

One hour and seventeen minutes. That's how long had passed since she'd left the voice mail.

One hour and two minutes. That's how long remained until John was allegedly coming over for pizza.

She'd tried to talk Andrew into letting her take him to the file, but he'd refused, said he wasn't about to let her lead him into a trap. Instead he was laying one, using her as bait.

"Maybe I should try again," she suggested. Make sure he knew. Make sure he understood. Restless, she started to stand, but with a single cold look from across the room, she eased back into the club chair. Andrew sat across from her, leaning forward with his elbows on his thighs, the gun pointed at her.

She'd expected him to tie her up, but he'd yet to lay a hand on her. It was almost as if—

As if he didn't want a single mark on her body.

"Why?" he asked. "Didn't you say you were supposed to call him and let him know where you'd be?"

Her throat tightened. "Yes."

"What's the matter then? Feeling sentimental? Guilty? Want to hear his voice one last time?"

One. Last. Time. "If you would just let me get the file on my own—"

"It wouldn't change a thing," he said mildly. "Detective D'Ambrosia was already a dead man when he woke up this morning. If you hadn't invited him to his execution, he would've bit it tonight. This just escalates my time frame."

Escalates. There was that word again.

Swallowing hard, Saura shoved the horror aside and stared at Andrew. She was still alive for a reason. He needed her for something, probably insurance or leverage, a bargaining chip to make sure John bent any direction Andrew wanted him to.

But she wasn't going to sit quietly by and let him get away with murder. Not even to himself.

"It was you, wasn't it?" She didn't try to hide the censure from her voice. "You said I killed your father…but it was you."

Something hard and brittle flickered in the gray of his eyes. "He couldn't see that you were using him. If you'd gone back inside with him…"

She could have blown everything sky-high. She'd been prepared. She'd had the sleeping pills, the camera. "He was your father," she whispered. "He was standing right next to me."

Andrew checked his watch. "I took tighter shots in the army."

"But you missed!"

"I had you all the way," he said in a voice stripped of emotion. "If that fool hadn't moved—"

"You're going to blame it on him?" Incredulity drove her. "Are you sure that wasn't your intent all along? You wanted to take his place, didn't you? Isn't that what this is about? Being better, doing more than he did."

The lines of his face tightened.

"You aim for me, but take him out instead—" She saw the flicker of emotion in his eyes. "Call it an accident, blame it on me, on him…go to bed with a clean conscience…"

His eyes hardened.

So she pushed harder. "Your father loved you."

"He loved the idea of me," Andrew shot back. "One weekend a month, two weeks a year, as long as I did what he wanted me to."

"He was trying to protect you." Never in a thousand years had she imagined she'd be defending Nathan Lambert.

But Andrew laughed. "He was trying to *stop* me. He said he'd do whatever it took. He was a scared old man who couldn't see that the world had changed, that the opportunity was endless. He was complacent, content to sit back and—"

"He would have taken the fall for you." The words tore from somewhere inside her. For over twenty-five years Nathan had eluded the authorities. He'd paid off cops and judges; he'd coerced and terrorized. But in the end, he would have taken the fall for his son…

"Maybe," Andrew said with an indifferent shrug. "But now that he's gone—and once you and the cop are gone—everyone will stop looking in my father's direction, won't they? They'll realize they were wrong."

The words chilled. Because they were true. Andrew would have carte blanche. No one would know.

"Not even your brother will look." He leaned closer, smiled wider. "He'll be grief-stricken, might even blame himself. He knows you've been going through a hard time. Maybe if he'd stayed home, watched over you instead of going off…"

Everything inside her stilled.

"He'll be haunted by the thought of the cop walking in and trying to stop you, of the struggle for the gun…of it going off."

Suicide. He was going to stage her suicide. But first, he was going to make it look as though she accidentally killed John.

"Once he was down…there was nothing to stop you from turning the gun on yourself."

Cain—God, Cain. Andrew was right. He would blame himself, torture himself. Losing Renee had almost killed him. "That's ridiculous," she hedged.

"Is it?" Andrew taunted. "Are you sure? Correct me if I'm wrong, but you won't be the first in your family, will you?"

People saw what they wanted to see, what made the most sense. Other than John, no one even knew she was investigating Lambert. And John, he was on leave. No one knew of his activities either. There would be no reason to link their deaths to the surge in black-market imports—just as there'd been nothing linking Gabe's father to anything shady.

"Uncle Troy did not kill himself," she said against the awful tightening inside.

"That's right." Andrew looked disgustingly amused. "You believe that nutcase cousin of yours, don't you? You think it was my father who shot your uncle in cold blood." His slow, controlling smile mocked. "Guess you believe the other rumors, too, about voodoo and stained glass windows that weep blood."

She didn't allow herself to move, not even as the odd glow in his eyes made something inside her shift. There'd been no motive, the sheriff had said. No reason for anyone to kill Troy Fontenot.

Finally, after over twenty years, Andrew Lambert had just filled in the last elusive blank.

"I don't know, what do you think?" she mused. "A piece of leaded glass smuggled out of southern France, a five-hundred-year-old depiction of the rapture, rumored to bleed when the sun hits it just so…" Now it was she who leaned forward. "Think someone might kill for that?" she asked, intrigued by the way Andrew straightened. "Think there might be a price for something like that on the black market?"

"You're as crazy as he was," he muttered. But the words were piercingly hollow. "If my father had given half as much attention to the future as he did the past—"

"What?" she pressed. "He would have realized it was a good thing to import shoddy pharmaceuticals? That there was a market for malnourished teenaged girls who can't speak the language, much less defend themselves? That it didn't matter who got hurt, so long as—"

The knock stopped her. She twisted toward the door with a hard slam of her heart, felt something hot and jagged rush through her. No, she wanted to scream. *No!*

Andrew surged to his feet and crossed the room, pointed his gun toward the entryway. She knew what she was to do now. She knew the plan. One misstep and John would pay the price before he even had a chance to react.

"Saura?" came John's voice, and the rhythm of her heart changed, deepened.

"It's open," she called. "Come on in."

The door pushed open and he was there, striding inside with a briefcase in one hand and a white paper bag in the other. He looked…normal. So ridiculously normal that she wanted to scream. With his blue jeans, long-sleeved black T-shirt and leather jacket he looked like any other man arriving for a night of takeout and videos. He even wore the earring. And cologne. The scent of leather and soap and man nearly broke her heart. There was not one sign that he knew, that he understood—except for the gleam in his eyes.

"Hope Chinese is okay," he said.

"Perfect," she said, but did not move. Couldn't move. Wasn't about to set Andrew off before John could assess.

He shut the door and strolled toward her. "Don't know about you, but I'm starved," he was saying. "I was hoping we could eat before tackling the file."

Her throat tightened, but somehow she smiled. "Stop," she said, and then Andrew was there, stepping into John's line of vision with his gun no longer trained on John, but on her.

"I'd listen to her if I were you," he said.

John froze. "Easy," he said.

Andrew stepped closer. "We'll see about that."

The cleft in John's chin deepened. He looked hard at her, promising without speaking, holding without moving, then like a shutter closing, his attention shifted to Andrew. "Let her go. I have what you need. No one needs to—"

Andrew laughed. "Don't mistake me for my father," he chided, gesturing toward the briefcase with his gun. "You can drop that now. And the paper bag." He watched while John obeyed. "Now your gun."

Saura's heart kicked hard. *No,* she wanted to scream, but with a calmness that chilled, John used his index finger to retrieve his Glock and toss it toward Andrew.

"Hands up," he said, and again, John obeyed. So completely calm. "Now put them on the wall," Andrew instructed, and again, John didn't argue, didn't even hesitate.

He had a plan. In that one fractured moment, Saura realized that more clearly than she'd ever realized anything.

Andrew stood five feet from her, not close enough for her to ram an elbow into his gut or stomp on his foot, do anything to distract him. And she knew why it had been so important that he not tie her up, not mar her in any way that would be incongruous with his tidy little murder/suicide plan.

"Get the briefcase," he barked, motioning with his gun.

Slowly she did. She glanced at John standing against the wall, his feet shoulder width apart, his palms splayed flat, and knew she had to do this for him. Had to do it right. Going down on one knee she opened the latches and flipped open the lid, stared at the contents. Keeping her breath steady, she picked everything up and slowly stood, turned toward Andrew.

"Take two steps," he said, and she realized he wasn't about to let her get any closer than that. Maybe he suspected.

"Now open the file," he said after she did as instructed,

and again, she obeyed, revealing the encrypted spreadsheet she'd recovered the night before. "Show it to me," he said.

That would be a little more difficult. Balancing the folder on one hand, she held up the page with her other hand—and saw the movement out of the corner of her eye. From the window.

Then everything shattered.

Andrew twisted toward the shower of glass, just as Cain stormed inside from the fire escape. She saw Andrew's gun lift and heard her brother shout, didn't stop to think. She drove forward and rammed the sharp rock John had placed in the briefcase into Andrew's bicep. His shot went wide, and then John was there, tackling Andrew and wrestling him to the ground, while Cain and two other men dressed in SWAT vests surged in from the blown-out window.

The single gunshot stopped her heart. For one horrible second everything froze. Then she was on her knees, lunging for where John and Andrew lay sprawled together. Cain dropped beside her and as they reached, John moved, pulled away from Andrew with a grim look in his eyes and no weapon in his hands. The SWAT-team members rolled Lambert's son over, revealed the gun in his hand and the blood oozing from his gut.

Then everything blurred. She saw John's mouth work, but heard nothing, was only aware of him crawling toward her, reaching for her and dragging her into his arms. She buried her face against his chest and felt the Kevlar, felt her throat tighten and her heart thrum. *"John."* Her *étranger*. She swallowed hard and held on tight, was vaguely aware of the way his hands ran along her back and tangled into her hair.

Lost in the moment, in him, it took a moment for the

fifth man to register. Tall. Grizzled. *Familiar.* She squinted against the fading sunlight pouring in through the shattered window. Then she blinked. *"Alec."*

"It was my father."

Standing in a puddle of soft yellow light on the porch of her family's ancestral home, Saura turned. She'd showered in the three hours since he'd last seen her, had changed into a pair of faded jeans and a soft pink sweater. Her long dark hair was loose, her face wiped clean of makeup.

John wasn't sure he'd ever seen her look more beautiful.

She didn't rush him, didn't say anything, as she watched him walk toward her through amazingly calm brown eyes.

His heart kicked anyway. "Earlier you asked me who died and took me with him…" The question had practically skewered him. Now he tightened his fingers around the silver discs in his hand. "Who died and made me a coward."

The unseasonably warm breeze blew hair into her face, but she made no move to brush it away.

"It was my father," he said, closing the distance between them. "I was eight years old."

Her eyes darkened, not with censure or horror, but with the warmth and compassion he'd come to crave. "John—"

Slowly he opened his fingers and stared down at his father's dog tags. "I didn't understand at first. Dads weren't supposed to die, not until their children were grown and had children of their own. But as I got older, I learned things." Found out details. Realized his dad's death could have been prevented. "And grief turned to anger. If Dad had been more careful— If he hadn't been thinking about my baseball game he was supposed to be at— If he and my mom hadn't argued the last time they'd spoken—" He bit off the words before he made a damn fool of himself. "I saw the wreckage he left in his wake, and I promised myself I would never do that. I wouldn't be like him. I'd be *better.*" He took a breath. "I'd do what he should have done."

He saw the moment she'd connected the dots. "Just like Andrew Lambert," he muttered.

The irony burned. Two sons. Both driven by their father's sins. One now lay dead. The other—

"No," Saura said, and finally she slid the hair back from her face, looked up at him with fire in her eyes. "Not like Andrew."

The urge to step closer, to pull her into his arms and never let go, almost sent him to his knees. "I was so determined to be untouched," he said instead, because damn it, she deserved to know. She deserved to understand. "To be on guard and to see everything, know everything…never get taken by surprise."

Her soft smile did just that. "That's what I saw in your eyes at Lucky's. The isolation—the cost of that isolation."

Something soft and thick squeezed around his heart. "I saw you, and it was like looking in a mirror." It still was. Through her, with her, he saw with a clarity he'd never before allowed. "I knew you were dangerous," he said, "but I couldn't stop coming back—couldn't stop wanting. I told myself I could kiss without tasting, touch without feeling…"

The warm breeze blew the hair back into her face. "Zero plus zero equals zero…"

"But I was wrong." Now he moved, couldn't remain isolated one second longer. "You— God, Saura, you touched me before you ever even crossed that barroom."

Stepping into him, she slid her arms around his waist. "I felt it, too."

"I looked for you—did you know that?" He wanted her to know. Needed her to. "I went back to Lucky's night after night, but you were never there."

Still smiling, she lifted a hand to his face and touched the cleft in his chin with her index finger.

"And then there you were, at the Mardi Gras party— with Nathan Lambert. Do you have any idea what it did to me to see you with him? To see you smiling at him and letting him touch you—"

"He never touched me," she said quietly. "Not like you do."

The emotion kept right on coming, hot, boiling streams of it. Driving him. "I'm a cop. I'm trained to look for motive and probable cause—"

"You thought I was on his payroll, that I'd gone after you at his behest."

"It made me sick," he admitted now, as he'd been unable to admit then. "And then I found out who you were—that you're Cain's sister, for crissakes, and that you'd been hurt. That your family was worried about you—"

"John." She pushed up on her toes and slid her hand to touch the side of his face. "You don't have to do this."

But he did. "I just wanted to make it better," he said, and now he was touching her, too; he had his hands on her face, his fingers against the soft warmth of her skin. "To make sure no one hurt you again, that Lambert didn't take you down with him. But then— Then everything changed, and all I could think about was you. Being with you. Touching you. Tasting—"

"More," she said, and the sparkle in her eyes damn near slayed him.

"More." That had been all he wanted. "And I thought I could have it, until this morning. I realized I'd violated every cardinal rule I'd set for myself. I'd failed, just like my father."

Her mouth feathered against his. "You didn't fail," she whispered. "*He* didn't fail."

Falling. It was an odd damn sensation. Always before he'd tried to stop himself. "I had to stop it," he tried to explain. "I had to cut it off. I thought if I let you walk away again, the blurriness would go away. That I could be that same focused cop I'd always been, that I wouldn't be distracted and you would be safe…"

"I was wrong when I called you a coward. What you did took more courage—"

"The hell it did." His voice was rough, but there was nothing rough about the way he wanted to touch her. "I took the easy way out and it damn near got you killed." Hold her. "Christ, Saura…look at you. Don't you think I know what it cost you to be with me?" Keep her. "Don't you think I know how much courage it took for you to let me in? And how did I repay that? By letting you walk away—"

"No," she said with a fierceness that surprised. "You can't think like that. It doesn't matter—"

And he couldn't just drown in her eyes, when he wanted to drown in her kiss. In her. "I love you, Saura," he said, taking her mouth with his own. "So damned much."

Against his cheek her fingers tightened. "I love you, too," she whispered, pulling back. "You know that, don't you?"

The words nearly cratered him. Somehow he'd never let himself imagine. Never let himself hope or dream. Now he never wanted to stop. "All I wanted was for you to stay," he said, threading his fingers through her hair. He held her as close as he could, knew he'd never be able to let go. *"For more."*

Her smile was soft, luminous. "Keep holding me like this," she murmured against his mouth, "and there will always, always be more."

* * * * *

Don't miss the next installment of the
MIDNIGHT SECRETS *miniseries!*
Be sure to catch Gabe's story,
A LITTLE BIT GUILTY
by Jenna Mills
Available June 2007
from Silhouette Romantic Suspense

Set in darkness beyond the ordinary world.
Passionate tales of life and death.
With characters' lives ruled by laws the
everyday world can't begin to imagine.

n o c t u r n e

It's time to discover the Raintree *trilogy...*

New York Times bestselling author
LINDA HOWARD
brings you the dramatic first book
RAINTREE: INFERNO

The Ansara Wizards are rising and the Raintree clan
must rejoin the battle against their foes, testing
their powers and relationships and forcing upon them
lives they never could have imagined before...

Turn the page for a sneak preview
of the captivating first book
in the Raintree *trilogy,*
RAINTREE: INFERNO by LINDA HOWARD
On sale April 2.

Dante Raintree stood with his arms crossed as he watched the woman on the monitor. The image was in black and white to better show details; color distracted the brain. He focused on her hands, watching every move she made, but what struck him most was how uncommonly *still* she was. She didn't fidget or play with her chips, or look around at the other players. She peeked once at her down card, then didn't touch it again, signaling for another hit by tapping a fingernail on the table. Just because she didn't seem to be paying attention to the other players, though, didn't mean she was as unaware as she seemed.

"What's her name?" Dante asked.

"Lorna Clay," replied his chief of security, Al Rayburn.

"At first I thought she was counting, but she doesn't pay enough attention."

"She's paying attention, all right," Dante murmured.

"You just don't see her doing it." A card counter had to remember every card played. Supposedly counting cards was impossible with the number of decks used by the casinos, but there were those rare individuals who could calculate the odds even with multiple decks.

"I thought that, too," said Al. "But look at this piece of tape coming up. Someone she knows comes up to her and speaks, she looks around and starts chatting, completely misses the play of the people to her left—and doesn't look around even when the deal comes back to her, just taps that finger. And damn if she didn't win. Again."

Dante watched the tape, rewound it, watched it again. Then he watched it a third time. There had to be something he was missing, because he couldn't pick out a single giveaway.

"If she's cheating," Al said with something like respect, "she's the best I've ever seen."

"What does your gut say?"

Al scratched the side of his jaw, considering. Finally, he said, "If she isn't cheating, she's the luckiest person walking. She wins. Week in, week out, she wins. Never a huge amount, but I ran the numbers and she's into us for about five grand a week. Hell, boss, on her way out of the casino she'll stop by a slot machine, feed a dollar in and walk away with at least fifty. It's never the same machine, either. I've had her watched, I've had her followed, I've even looked for the same faces in the casino every time she's in here, and I can't find a common denominator."

"Is she here now?"

"She came in about half an hour ago. She's playing blackjack, as usual."

"Bring her to my office," Dante said, making a swift decision. "Don't make a scene."

"Got it," said Al, turning on his heel and leaving the security center.

Dante left, too, going up to his office. His face was calm. Normally he would leave it to Al to deal with a cheater, but he was curious. How was she doing it? There were a lot of bad cheaters, a few good ones, and every so often one would come along who was the stuff of which legends were made: the cheater who didn't get caught, even when people were alert and the camera was on him— or, in this case, her.

It was possible to simply be lucky, as most people understood luck. Chance could turn a habitual loser into a big-time winner. Casinos, in fact, thrived on that hope. But luck itself wasn't habitual, and he knew that what passed for luck was often something else: cheating. And there was the other kind of luck, the kind he himself possessed, but it depended not on chance but on who and what he was. He knew it was an innate power and not Dame Fortune's erratic smile. Since power like his was rare, the odds made it likely the woman he'd been watching was merely a very clever cheat.

Her skill could provide her with a very good living, he thought, doing some swift calculations in his head. Five grand a week equaled $260,000 a year, and that was just from his casino. She probably hit them all, careful to keep the numbers relatively low so she stayed under the radar.

He wondered how long she'd been taking him, how long she'd been winning a little here, a little there, before Al noticed.

The curtains were open on the wall-to-wall window in

his office, giving the impression, when one first opened the door, of stepping out onto a covered balcony. The glazed window faced west, so he could catch the sunsets. The sun was low now, the sky painted in purple and gold. At his home in the mountains, most of the windows faced east, affording him views of the sunrise. Something in him needed both the greeting and the goodbye of the sun. He'd always been drawn to sunlight, maybe because fire was his element to call, to control.

He checked his internal time: four minutes until sundown. Without checking the sunrise tables every day, he knew exactly when the sun would slide behind the mountains. He didn't own an alarm clock. He didn't need one. He was so acutely attuned to the sun's position that he had only to check within himself to know the time. As for waking at a particular time, he was one of those people who could tell himself to wake at a certain time, and he did. That talent had nothing to do with being Raintree, so he didn't have to hide it; a lot of perfectly ordinary people had the same ability.

He had other talents and abilities, however, that did require careful shielding. The long days of summer instilled in him an almost sexual high, when he could feel contained power buzzing just beneath his skin. He had to be doubly careful not to cause candles to leap into flame just by his presence, or to start wildfires with a glance in the dry-as-tinder brush. He loved Reno; he didn't want to burn it down. He just felt so damn *alive* with all the sunshine pouring down that he wanted to let the energy pour through him instead of holding it inside.

This must be how his brother Gideon felt while pulling lightning, all that hot power searing through his muscles, his veins. They had this in common, the connection with raw power. All the members of the far-flung Raintree clan had some power, some heightened ability, but only members of the royal family could channel and control the earth's natural energies.

Dante wasn't just of the royal family, he was the Dranir, the leader of the entire clan. "Dranir" was synonymous with king, but the position he held wasn't ceremonial, it was one of sheer power. He was the oldest son of the previous Dranir, but he would have been passed over for the position if he hadn't also inherited the power to hold it.

Behind him came Al's distinctive knock on the door. The outer office was empty, Dante's secretary having gone home hours before. "Come in," he called, not turning from his view of the sunset.

The door opened, and Al said, "Mr. Raintree, this is Lorna Clay."

Dante turned and looked at the woman, all his senses on alert. The first thing he noticed was the vibrant color of her hair, a rich, dark red that encompassed a multitude of shades from copper to burgundy. The warm amber light danced along the iridescent strands, and he felt a hard tug of sheer lust in his gut. Looking at her hair was almost like looking at fire, and he had the same reaction.

The second thing he noticed was that she was spitting mad.

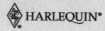

EVERLASTING LOVE™

Every great love has a story to tell ™

If you're a romantic at heart, you'll definitely want to read this new series.

Available April 24

The Marriage Bed by Judith Arnold

An emotional story about a couple's love that is put to the test when the shocking truth of a long-buried secret comes to the surface.

&

Family Stories by Tessa McDermid

A couple's epic love story is pieced together by their granddaughter in time for their seventy-fifth anniversary.

And look for

The Scrapbook by Lynnette Kent

&

When Love Is True by Joan Kilby

from Harlequin® Everlasting Love™ this June.

Pick up a book today!

www.eHarlequin.com

HELMAY07

Silhouette®

ROMANTIC
SUSPENSE

**Sparked by Danger,
Fueled by Passion.**

**This month and every month look for
four new heart-racing romances
set against a backdrop of suspense!**

Available in May 2007

Safety in Numbers
(Wild West Bodyguards miniseries)
by Carla Cassidy

Jackson's Woman
by Maggie Price

Shadow Warrior
(Night Guardians miniseries)
by Linda Conrad

One Cool Lawman
by Diane Pershing

Available wherever you buy books!

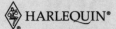
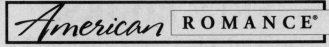

REQUEST YOUR FREE BOOKS!

2 FREE NOVELS PLUS 2 FREE GIFTS!

Silhouette® Romantic

SUSPENSE

Sparked by Danger, Fueled by Passion!

YES! Please send me 2 FREE Silhouette® Romantic Suspense novels and my 2 FREE gifts. After receiving them, if I don't wish to receive any more books, I can return the shipping statement marked "cancel." If I don't cancel, I will receive 4 brand-new novels every month and be billed just $4.24 per book in the U.S., or $4.99 per book in Canada, plus 25¢ shipping and handling per book plus applicable taxes, if any*. That's a savings of at least 15% off the cover price! I understand that accepting the 2 free books and gifts places me under no obligation to buy anything. I can always return a shipment and cancel at any time. Even if I never buy another book from Silhouette, the two free books and gifts are mine to keep forever.

240 SDN EEX6 340 SDN EEYJ

Name	(PLEASE PRINT)
Address	Apt. #
City	State/Prov.	Zip/Postal Code

Signature (if under 18, a parent or guardian must sign)

Mail to the **Silhouette Reader Service™:**
IN U.S.A.: P.O. Box 1867, Buffalo, NY 14240-1867
IN CANADA: P.O. Box 609, Fort Erie, Ontario L2A 5X3

Not valid to current Silhouette Intimate Moments subscribers.

Want to try two free books from another line?
Call 1-800-873-8635 or visit www.morefreebooks.com.

* Terms and prices subject to change without notice. NY residents add applicable sales tax. Canadian residents will be charged applicable provincial taxes and GST. This offer is limited to one order per household. All orders subject to approval. Credit or debit balances in a customer's account(s) may be offset by any other outstanding balance owed by or to the customer. Please allow 4 to 6 weeks for delivery.

Your Privacy: Silhouette is committed to protecting your privacy. Our Privacy Policy is available online at www.eHarlequin.com or upon request from the Reader Service. From time to time we make our lists of customers available to reputable firms who may have a product or service of interest to you. If you would prefer we not share your name and address, please check here. ☐

SRS07

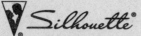

Silhouette®
Romantic
SUSPENSE

COMING NEXT MONTH